Fiona Hammond was born in Glasgow, moved to Berkshire and then Australia, before settling back in the UK. She worked for 15 years in social services, before graduating from the John Morris Journalism Academy and becoming a freelance journalist. Currently, she resides in rural Oxfordshire with her husband, daughters and friendly felines.

Dedication

For Ezme and Mia.
With thanks to the Mcachems.

07795 849376

Fiona Hammond

FLAKE

AUSTIN MACAULEY PUBLISHERS™

LONDON * CAMBRIDGE * NEW YORK * SHARJAH

A CIP catalogue record for this title is available from the British Library.

ISBN 9781786121677 (Paperback)
ISBN 9781786121684 (Hardback)
ISBN 9781786121691 (E Book)

www.austinmacauley.com

First Published (2018)
Austin Macauley Publishers Ltd.
25 Canada Square
Canary Wharf
London
E14 5LQ

Prologue

Ian urged the car faster down the narrow country lane. "God let me be on time... don't let me be too late." The woman sitting in the passenger seat turned a white face towards him.

"I can see the house." Breaking in front of an open gate both doors flew open and the occupants jumping from the car raced up the path, stopping at the front door. Ian stood to the side and gently pushed, the door swung inwards; moonlight illuminated the blackness of the hall giving the walls and floor a silvery sheen. They made their way quickly and silently towards the orangey glow escaping from the half open door at the end of the hall.

Ian pushed the door fully open and the woman at his side gasped and covered her mouth with her hand; a young man sat in the middle of the floor in a pool of blood and excrement. He cradled the head of a woman in his arms, rocking backwards and forwards he said over and over: "I didn't know what to do... I covered her up... it's okay mum... you're okay."

Ian knelt by his side and felt for the woman's pulse; it fluttered weakly under his fingers. She turned her head and whispered huskily gasping between each syllable in pain. He lowered his head to hers, "He... can't... live... Ian... didn't talk... Ness... hide Ness," her head fell backwards and she was gone.

The young man gently laid his mother down in the pool of her own blood. The stench was nauseating... blood oozed through the table cloth he had covered her with, he didn't want to look at what was under the cloth ever again... his mother's bowel had been laid at her side and feet her breasts had been almost completely hacked away, between her legs was a mass of blood and raw flesh everything had been systematically cut away...he stood up and racing to the back door hauled it open, lurched outside and vomited.

He was back in within minutes. Ian had just hung up on a call. The young man stood in front of him, his face grey, his eyes bloodshot, he opened his mouth to speak but nothing happened. He tried again, "Ness... where's my sister?"

They found her. Alive, unharmed, with her hands pressed tight to her eyes, she was huddled in the gap between the wall and the shelf in the cupboard under the sink. She didn't speak, didn't blink, she wrapped her arms around her brothers neck and clung to him for dear life, he held her tightly shielding her face from their mother's body and carried her to Ian's car and sat in the back still holding tightly to her, staring straight ahead of him.

Within half an hour Ian and the woman were back in the car and the house was swarming with people, unmarked cars and an ambulance stood in the lane.

"Ian," he turned to the young man.

"I know what you and mum do... I want a job... I'm going to hunt the bastard down...."

Chapter One

You cannot hope to bribe or twist,

Thank god! The British journalist.

But seeing what the man will do

Unbribed, there's no occasion to.

– *Humbert Wolfe, The Uncelestial city*

Ness Gordon came to with a start as the train slowed to a juddering halt. Wiping the steamy window with her jacket sleeve she looked out onto the one-platform Victorian station; the rain was coming down in heavy sheets as she peered through the murky glass, just able to read the sign swinging in the wind.

"Hell! That's my stop," slinging her bag round her neck and grabbing her small case from the floor she ran for the door, winding the window down, her hand fumbling outside for the lock.

At the same time the train jerked into movement, the door flew open and Ness fell onto the platform, her suitcase skidding across the wet brick. A plump and irritable guard lumbered heavily towards the swinging door slamming it shut with a mumbled "Bloody fool."

"I'm fine just in case you cared!" she shouted after the guard adding in an undertone "Wanker."

"Would it be Miss Gordon?" a soft highland accent enquired.

Ness looked up from the station floor and followed a pair of legs encased in thick tweed topped with a heavy rain coat and finished with a large waterproof hat. The wrinkled face under the hat was smiling and wore the biggest handlebar moustache – grey with a few bright ginger flecks – that Ness had seen. Bright blue eyes sparkled down at her as a hand was extended in an offer to help her up.

"Yes. I'm Ness Gordon," sitting in a swelling puddle Ness took the proffered hand, it had surprising strength, she noted, as she was pulled to her feet.

"Glad to make your acquaintance Miss Gordon, best be getting you back to the house so you can change out of those wet things. If you'll just follow me the car is waiting outside."

Grabbing her suitcase and falling into step, Ness cleared her throat

"Um… Sir John Woldarc, is it?"

"That's right, here we are then," Sir John took the case and dropped it lightly into the back of the four wheel drive as Ness climbed into the front seat, glad to be out of the stinging rain.

The road wound its way out from the station, fields of bleating sheep huddling together in defence against the harsh weather stood either side. In the distance, proud and unbending, were forests of large Scottish pine; just visible through the trees was the dark red brick of a turreted house.

Sir John stopped at a fork in the road pointing to the left.

"A mile that way is the village: a few shops, post office and pub. Most people take the train or drive into town if they need anything major." He took the right turn, driving on through the pines and passing a small cottage next to two large metal ornate gates, up a long sweeping driveway. The car came to rest outside what looked like a Gothic castle.

Sir John nimbly swung himself from the car and, retrieving the suitcase from the back, joined Ness who was out of the car staring up open mouthed at the gothic pile in front of her. Sir John, mistaking her look for coveted reverence, nodded to her, "Yes, impressive isn't she... been in the family for generations." He nodded in the general direction of the double black medieval oak doors and Ness, interpreting him correctly, followed.

On the other side of the doors three black rounded stone steps lead down into a black and white tiled hall. Ornate black lead and glass lamps hung from the walls and a large winding staircase lead to the next floor.

Portraits of the Woldarc family ancestors hung from the walls, all staring down at Ness in various haughty poses, some astride horses charging into battle and some with tartan slung across their shoulders and a foot atop a slaughtered deer. The woman all had heaving bosoms, showing more cleavage and nipple than would now be considered decent.

Ness came out of her reverie, aware she was being addressed, "This is Agnes Pike, our housekeeper. Agnes will show you to your room, Miss Gordon. Supper is at eight, and please feel free to rest or explore. I won't expect you to start work until the morrow."

Sir John, having given Agnes charge of Ness and her suitcase, left for his study and a stiff whiskey to drive out the cold.

"Follow me please, Miss," Agnes was tall and thin with pinched cheeks. Her dark hair was scraped back tightly into a bun and held in place with various large and painful looking pins. She was all angles and sharp lines – her shrewd blue eyes were as sharp as the elbows poking out of her black cardigan and her stiff apron rustled as she walked.

"How long have you worked for Sir John, Agnes?"

"Over twenty years, Miss."

"Please call me Ness. You must have started very young."

"I did."

Ness waited for more to follow. She had the impression this stick thin, sour housekeeper didn't like her, but it could just be that her character matched her body: sharp.

When the silence became too much for Ness to bear, she tried again.

"Are there any other staff, Agnes?"

"Two gardener's, the gilly, a cook, Sir John's personal assistant and estate manager and two ladies who come up from the village every day to do the heavy cleaning, but I don't expect you'll have much to do with them, Miss."

They had stopped outside a thick wooden door. Agnes pushed it open to reveal a bright and comfortable looking bedroom with a cheery fire already lit. She put the suitcase on the floor and crossed the room to another door, opening it to reveal a bathroom with bath and over bath shower.

"You'll find everything you need in here, Miss, if you would like to freshen up after your journey," she looked at Ness' bedraggled appearance with marked disgust before adding, "Will there be anything else?"

Ness, short tempered at the best of times, was beginning to feel like the bastard child of the country squire; definitely not welcome but to be shown as much courtesy as her position derived. She was cold, hungry and in dire need of a strong coffee and a cigarette or three and her patience was definitely wearing thin with the angular sour housekeeper.

"I would love a coffee please... Mrs Pike, if it's not too much trouble for you," she smiled noting with satisfaction the 'Mrs Pike' hadn't gone unnoticed.

Red in the face Agnes crossed to a dresser pointing to a kettle cafeteria and mugs sitting on a tray. Opening a dresser door she revealed a flask of cool milk, ground coffee, teabags and a tin of biscuits.

"Everything is here, Miss, help yourself. We'll see you downstairs at 8pm; Sir John likes dinner to be prompt," Agnes walked stiffly to the door closing it firmly behind her.

Ness stuck her finger up at the closed door before locking it and switched the kettle on.

Taking her mobile out of her padded jacket pocket Ness began a text. 'ARRIVED SAFE AND VERY WET. CALL YOU LATER. N.'

By the time Ness had filled the coffee jug and found with a yelp of happiness a small balcony outside her bedroom that was reachable via the long window which meant she could smoke, her mobile beeped a reply. 'GREAT. SPEAK LATER. BE CAREFUL. P.'

Ness snorted. Yeah that'll be right. Be careful but come back with the story or don't come back, was her editors' usual missive. Still, Ness mused, she loved her job as an investigative journalist and if her contact was right, then she, Ness Gordon was about to embark on the scoop of her career. First impressions of Sir John didn't lend much weight to the information that he was actually a Russian agent, had been since the early 70's and – if all was to believed – had the blood of many innocents on his hands and Britain's secret service had lost operatives solely to the information he supplied to Moscow. Apparently he was one of their favourite spies. Not bad for a peer of the realm. Ness yawned and smiled nastily: his housekeeper she could see in that role easily. Ah well, time would tell, thought Ness as she gratefully sank into the hot bubble bath she had run.

Lucky for them he was writing his memoirs and needed a freelance ghost writer to help him do it, lucky too, she thought as her eyes slowly closed, that she had the experience to apply and the contacts to recommend her for the position.

Dinner that evening was an odd affair. Ness had managed to find the dining room at five minutes to eight and was dutifully seated by Sir John, served albeit gruffly by Agnes dressed in a crisp black high necked dress.

Agnes hadn't seen fit to tell her that dinner dress was expected of guests. Ness was glad she had worn one of the few dresses she had brought with her. A clinging, just below the knee, jumper dress in jade green that accentuated every curve and added lustre to her long auburn wavy hair. A pair of simple black two inch heels gave her 5ft 10 inch frame greater stature. Sir John's personal assistant slash estate manager Ewan certainly couldn't keep his eyes off her.

Ewan was the only other diner and conversation stayed mostly to the running of the estate. Cautious looks between Agnes and her employer made Ness wonder if there had been some household disagreement and when Agnes thumped dessert down in front of Ness she realised whatever it was probably had involved herself.

Thanking Agnes sweetly for her bowl of apple crumble and cream she turned her hazel eyes with flecks of green back to Ewan who was enthusiastically offering to show her around the estate when they both had free time.

"I would love to, thanks for the offer Ewan, if the estate is as amazing as the house it will be something to look forward to. When we have the time of course," Ness smiled over at Sir John who agreed wholeheartedly.

"Well if you'll excuse us, Miss Gordon," Sir John rose and so did Ewan, the latter reluctantly peeling his eyes from Ness' breasts.

"I'll see you at 10am in my study."

"Yes 10am sharp, Sir John. Goodnight," then as if in an afterthought "would it be okay if I explored the grounds? I could do with a walk after the long train journey and it looks as if the rain is off for the night."

"Whatever you like, Miss Gordon You'll be needing wellington boots. If you have none with you I'm sure Agnes can find you a pair that fit," Sir John smiled and left the room with Ewan who looked rather like a puppy refused a walk. On their way past Agnes, Sir John gave her a meaningful look which Agnes returned with surprising animosity for an employee. Twenty minutes later Ness, dressed in jeans, a jumper and red wellington boots, walked slowly through the grounds smoking a cigarette.

All around her was the smell of pine and freshly rained on earth, the July evening – now the rain had stopped – was glorious. The sun hadn't fully sunk in the sky and it looked as if one of the two gardeners was taking full advantage of the summer evening planting out one of the many flower beds.

Ness smiled and said good evening to the muscular, T-shirted back as she passed wondering if she should try and walk to the village, check out the pub. By the time she had got to the end of the driveway her long day had caught up with her and knowing she still had some research to do before she turned in, lit another cigarette instead and headed back to the house.

The gardener was still there, talking into his mobile, one mud stained hand running through his thick black hair. As Ness approached he turned his back slightly and she heard his voice raise a little as if arguing with someone. Ness smiled, poor bloke, she thought, lovers' tiff it sounded like.

Her own mobile then rang. Looking down at the name on the screen: 'Kalum' was lit up.

Great, she thought, what did her big brother want, or more to the point, what had she done to upset him? Kalum was fourteen years her senior and though she was twenty six he still treated her as if she was a rebellious teenager. Then again, she mused, not many big brothers would take on a six year old girl because their mother did a runner one night, never to be heard of again.

Before she could get the words 'Hi Kal,' out of her mouth, her brother's deep voice, angry at her, just for a change, boomed in her ear.

"What the fuck are you doing?"

"Um, listening to you shout."

"Don't you dare play games with me Ness!"

"Kal, mate, I don't know what the fuck you're on about."

"Are you working for Sir John?"

"Yup."

"Leave now!"

"Nope," Ness moved toward the drive again, scared of being overheard. She didn't want to blow her cover, passing the gardener she rolled her eyes at him, gestured to the phone with her free hand and said so Kal could hear. "Irrational older brother, suffers from separation anxiety, take a blue pill sweetie," and she hung up.

Ness messaged her editor at *The Globe.* 'HOW DID KAL KNOW? CALL ME NOW. N.' Her mobile rang within minutes of Ness reaching her room. Locking herself in the bathroom to take it, she said, "Phil... if you didn't tell him I was here, how the hell did he know and why was he so hot under his starchy collar? Do you think he knows Sir John? If so, that could spell trouble for us... if my cover is blown by my pen pushing brother we've lost the scoop of the year," Ness listened as Phil interjected firmly that he couldn't afford to attract bad press for a botched attempt to dish the dirt, albeit dirt that needed to be dished on a peer of the realm and a respected moneyed member of the community. He was sure he did not need to remind Ness that Sir John Woldarc had friends in high places therefore tangible proof was his and Ness' golden ticket. He did not also need to remind Ness that there were other journalists that would bite their own hands off for this assignment, and if she felt she was unable to deal with it just tell him now and come home.

"Just send me the bloody files through, Phil, and if my brother calls you tell him I'm on leave... I'll say

I'm moonlighting for extra cash... saving for a trip of a lifetime... yeah Phil, I know; be careful but come home with the goods or don't come home." Bastard! Ness made herself a mug of tea and had a cigarette on the balcony, waiting for Phil to send the information they had on Sir John and his relationship with Vladimir не мне, Russian leader, through her smart phone. Ness had a quiet giggle. How the hell was she supposed to take a guy named after a vampire seriously whilst she worked for his side kick in a Gothic monstrosity?

Chapter Two

I saw something nasty in the woodshed!

Sure you did, but did it see you?

– *Stella Gibbons, Cold Comfort Farm*

Kalum Gordon paced the office, hands clenched into fists by his side. It was 9.30pm but it could have been am for the amount of activity that was going on in the building of SIS. It was an organisation that never slept they didn't keep ordinary hours and most of their friends and family didn't truly know who they worked for.

Maybe it was time, thought Kal, to come clean with his baby sister. He was, after all, entitled to tell one family member the truth about his job. Their mother had chosen him as person of contact in her time and that hadn't worked out well, hell! Ness didn't even know the truth about their mum.

The organisation gave their employees cover stories to satisfy everyone else and he had decided to stick with his when it came to Ness... but, he argued with himself, that was twenty years ago and his kid sister still thought he was an anal retentive pen pusher.

The intercom on the desk buzzed. Kalum dropped his 6ft 4 muscular frame into the leather swivel chair and irritably demanded "What?"

"Big boss on his way Kal, you better not be in his chair."

"Shit."

Kalum pulled himself out of the soft leather and continued his pacing, the office door opened.

"Gordon you look like a prowling lion about to devour its prey, sit down, calm down and tell me why your sister is suddenly up to her eyeballs in this mess."

The new and youthful small blonde secretary who had teetered in after the chief looked almost hungrily at Kalum's rippling thigh muscles, held tightly in a pair of black jeans, crisp black hair protruded invitingly out of the top of his open white collared shirt which held the promise of a hard warmth beneath. His long legs stretched out in front of him lazily fallen apart gave her a view of his crotch that she found mesmerising.

The chief coughed "Miss Fanshaw... coffee. Hot, strong and lots of it... please."

Kalum grinned up at her as she left, "Just like me."

The intercom buzzed again, "Yes."

"Mark, for you and Kal sir."

The chief pressed a button "Go," Kalum leant forward and pulled his chair nearer to the desk, "where is she?"

"On a balcony outside her room, she's reading something on her phone and not looking too happy about it... oh yeah,, and she smokes far too much, you should tell her it's bad for her, mate."

Their chief interrupted, "Has she ever met you before?"

"Once... barbeque at Kal's... few years ago... she was a bit pissed... hasn't recognised me."

"Keep a close eye but do not compromise yourself."

"Sir."

"Mark."

"Yes Kal."

"A close eye... that's all... am I clear?"

"Sure thing mate... you know me where a pretty ladies involved."

Kal banged his fist on the table and shouted at the intercom

"For fuck's sake Mark!"

"Gordon that's enough!" interrupting the flow their boss continued.

"A close eye Mark... try and find out what she has on the target and do not let her find out who you are... check in every 24 hours. Before if there's news, and for Kal's sake... keep her safe... I really don't think she knows who or what she's dealing with."

"Yes sir, and Kal, mate... I didn't mean it... about the woman thing, besides there's a nice bit in the village who fancies me rotten."

The chief switched off the intercom before Kal's temper could rise to Marks well-meaning but badly timed teasing. He knew the two men well, they had each other's backs no matter what it seemed to outsiders. He also knew that Marks ill-timed tomfooleries were meant wholly to allay Kal's fears for Ness.

The young and now red-faced secretary brought in a tray of coffee and not meeting either of the men's eyes, left again.

They sat in silence whilst Kal poured coffee for both of them, the chief mused some more on the current situation. In his opinion Kal had spoiled Ness rotten... tried to make up for too much that wasn't his fault... let her have to long a leash when she was growing up... overcompensation... a few well timed slaps to her spoiled backside would not have gone amiss... maybe it's not too late. He put down his coffee cup and motioned to Kal for a refill.

"Gordon."

"Sir."

"Can I ask a personal question?"

"Fire away."

"When Ness was growing up... how did you discipline her?"

"You think I spoilt her... don't answer, Sir... I did, I suppose, just couldn't bring myself to punish her... I threatened it but never carried it through... bit too late to lock her in her room now though."

About ten years too late if Ness' file was to be believed and the chief had no reason to doubt it... Kalum seemed to be oblivious to the majority of its contents. He supposed he was to blame for that, he had shielded Ness as much as Kal and what's probably worse, shielded Kal from the worst of Ness' behaviour. Guilty conscience? He supposed so. A lot of the old team had reason to share guilt after what happened to their mum, his friend and co-worker. Ness had been in the house that night... couldn't remember a thing... didn't know the truth, and that's where her behaviour over the years stemmed from; they all knew that. Maybe it was time that all changed... she was, after all, in the home of the man

26

who had tortured and killed her mother... one or the other would remember sooner or later and it was of vital importance that Ness recognised and listened to authority... her life would depend upon it. He had come to a decision.

Reaching into a desk drawer he placed a file on the top and pushed it toward Kalum. Kalum glanced at the name on the binder, that his sister was on file was no surprise – that it was locked in his boss's desk was.

"You need to read this, digest it and then we move on."

Kalum read for over an hour. By the time he had finished, he was enraged; a blue vein was pulsing in his forehead.

"You kept... all of this... from me," he said, through gritted teeth.

"What would you have done if you had known? Sent her for more counselling? You have to make her listen to you... for once. I'll make arrangements for you to travel up, probably better having you closer to the target, and you have to get Ness on board or out of there. He held out his hand to take the file back which Kalum grudgingly handed over before striding out of the room, slamming the door hard behind him.

The chief could hear him yelling orders at subordinates all the way down the hall, he pressed the intercom "Get me Mark," best let him know a storm was coming.

Ian, known to his team as the Big Boss or Chief, sat back in the large leather chair waiting for Mark to call in. Automatically reaching into his desk for a cigarette before he remembered he had just given up. He had promised his wife he would before he retired, she didn't want him to fall off his perch just when she didn't have to share him with anyone else.

Bugger it, he thought, lighting one up. Moving across to the high window, blowing smoke through his nose and gazing onto the brightly lit streets below, he thought how things had changed over the years. There was a time that no one knew where their offices were, let alone acknowledged what they did in them, what they directed from them. Now everyone knew where they were... film companies could hire parts of it to make movies... granted it was normally only the frontage... but still... hell, they even advertised on the fucking internet... used to be the back page of the times... still was. He took another grateful drag on his cigarette watching the traffic move slowly towards London Bridge, the orange and red glow of lights contributed a soothing radiance through the swirling mist that had started to hover above the river and seep onto the street below. He had always found it strangely calming, watching people doing ordinary everyday things. He snorted, his PA told him it made him a bit of a stalker... that always made him laugh... she couldn't know that was his code name a long time ago.

He took a last drag, noting he had smoked his cigarette down to the filter, stubbing what was left out, he dragged his gaze from the street below and the herds of sheep-like people, that's just what they were at times. Herds. Easy to manipulate, to whip up into a frenzy of imprudent protest. Typically directed toward those who put their lives on the line so they could continue theirs uninterrupted... sleep safely in their beds... that fucking little traitorous wanker Snowden had done his best to whip them into a frenzy... succeeded, too... Protests contrary to their own safety, against his and others organisations for infringing the public's privacy and freedom of speech. The very same establishments that protected their country's freedom and its protesting populous, Ian's lip curled into a menacing sneer. Freedom and privacy. Two things that were hard won privileges... not won by the vast majority of the sheep bleating against them being trespassed... not for the first time he wondered at the crass stupidity of the frenzied mob... did they honestly think that what most of them had to say was of any interest or importance to anyone else? He wondered why very few had stopped to consider if it was only mass surveillance Snowden was concerned about, why he had stolen millions of other secrets... secrets that had put lives of their fellow countrymen in danger... in some cases had extinguished them... very few had questioned his connection with Russia and therefore не мне... Snowden... whatever he was promised, he will have realised too late it was total bollocks; if he's smart he will and that guy is no idiot.

The intercom buzzed. "Mark on the line, Sir."

"About fucking time, where have you been... no don't answer that, I can imagine."

"Sorry Sir, I couldn't pick up... Ness made an idiotic attempt to get into his study... I had to fire off a few shots... that Ewan dickhead dashed out... told them I was after a fox... it was enough to get her bolting back upstairs though."

"Shit! Was she seen?"

"No, Sir."

"Gordon's on his way up, we've hired a holiday cottage for a month, he's a solicitor there with his wife for a holiday, she's a romance writer getting the background for an historical novel set in the highlands. Driving up tonight, arrive tomorrow morning."

"Who's the lucky lady?"

"Max."

"What are you going to do without her?"

"Needs must Mark... Fanshaw will fill in... and let's face it do you know anyone else who could pass off as a convincing writer of historical romances within the next six hours?"

"No, Sir... er... good choice."

"I wasn't seeking your approval Mark. Another thing, I've had to inform Gordon about a few details... concerning Ness that he wasn't aware of before... he's... well... angry doesn't cover it... Ness is in his direct line of fire."

"Want me to buffer?"

"No! I want you to leave him well alone when he faces her... she needs whatever he dishes out... skeletons will be leaving closets... just don't get in his way when they do... don't rush to her defence... no matter how he decides to handle her...it is of the utmost importance that Ness listens to, and takes direction from, him... there's too much at stake... we can't lose the target due to a hag ridden editor and I won't lose any of my team to a young woman's stupidity."

"Got it, Sir."

"Good... Gordon will be in touch."

Ian flicked the intercom off and then back on. "Max."

"Sir."

"You ready to go?"

"Off in five."

"Be careful Max... Gordon and Mark will have your back... don't let Ness get under your skin... don't feel sympathy... let Gordon handle it... er, Max?"

"Yes, Sir?"

"Your husband okay about this?"

"Fine… he's taking the boys to his mother's in Spain for a fortnight, they won't have time to miss me."

"Thanks, Max."

"Welcome, Sir."

Ian reached out for another smoke, his wife was going to smell it on him anyway, may as well be hung for a sheep, as a lamb.

What to do about Ness' editor? The guy was a known tosser, Ian had good mates that were seasoned journalists and had had dealings through work with an editor or two, none of them would push a newbie into known danger like this… he'd have to put him on the back burner… letting Phil know they knew would only confirm his story and hand him a great headline to splatter across the tabloids… but he would come back to him.

He'd convince Ness to try somewhere else… she was a good writer but her career would be over before it began under Phil's inept leadership… the wanker was only interested in greasing his own slimy palm.

Stubbing his cigarette out, Ian brushed a little fallen ash from his suit front and made ready to leave for home… the boys would call in if anything was needed before tomorrow and apart from anything else he was dog tired... retirement... never thought he would admit it... but it was looking better every day

Chapter Three

When you destroy a blade of grass

You poison England at her roots:

Remember no man's foot can pass

Where evermore no green life shoots.

– *Gordon Bottomley, To Iron-Founders and Others*

Ness woke the following morning feeling tired and grubby, still in the same position; huddled on her bed fully clothed. The first thing her eyes fell on was the chair she had wedged under the door handle last night or, to be accurate, this morning.

Bloody stupid thing to do, she thought in hindsight, leaving the breaking and entering until she knew the household movements would have been the professional thing to do... then again how was she supposed to know that the idiot gardener would be out shooting at foxes in the dead of night... quick thinking on her part... pretending she was coming out of her room rather than going in when Ewan had hurtled out of nowhere, just as her hand had made contact with the door handle... she hadn't missed the gun shoved hastily behind his back. Ness smiled maliciously, the helpless female act was always so easy when the mark fancied you; always got you out of trouble.

Ness had a shower, removed the chair from the door and was taking a large pot of coffee onto the balcony when there was a knock. Opening the door revealed a hastily deposited breakfast tray. Ness took that out onto the balcony and after her usual three cigarettes for breakfast got stuck into bacon and eggs, washed down with orange juice. She enjoyed the novelty as she chewed over the files Phil had sent through late last night. The hard thing... she acknowledged to herself whilst lighting another cigarette, was to remain on friendly terms with Sir John and not to let what she had read about the bastard show on her face... wouldn't hurt to get more info on Ewan. She'd have to find out his second name and get a photo of him on her smart phone, send it all off to Phil and see what he can dig up. Okay time to get to work... she'd arrive a little early; never know what you can overhear waiting outside a door, and if the door opened whilst she was listening, she'd just pretend to knock.

Feeling confidant with her own cunning, Ness made her way downstairs, careful to ask Agnes as she passed her on the stairs which way the study was to be found. "The left passage from the dining room, door at the end, Miss. I thought you knew."

The housekeeper's shrewd eye was unnerving, "Thanks, Mrs Pike... my sense of direction is not the best."

"No, Miss? I thought you managed quite well last night."

Ness stopped in her tracks... don't rise to the bait, the old bitch is just fishing... turning slowly on the stairs to face Agnes who stood duster in hand, all sharpness and cunning. Ness laughed.

"Can't exactly get lost walking down the drive, but I would like to go into town one day... maybe you could show me the way?"

Not waiting for a reply Ness carried on down the stairs, feeling the house keeper's eyes burn into her back as she went.

Agnes would be heading straight for Ness's room; that she was sure of, and with a look of cunning not unlike the housekeeper's she smiled; nothing to find up there. Ness patted her pocket where her smart phone lay safely along with her wallet. She was always very careful not to leave anything incriminating laying around.

Turning down the corridor towards the study Ness fingered the heavy oak walled panelling, looking with disdain at the stags' heads mounted onto brass plaques. Although there was a large window at the end of the corridor it let in little light as it was hung with long heavy blood red curtains and added to Ness's overall feeling that she had stepped onto a Gothic horror film set.

Ness checked her watch: ten minutes to go. Leaning in a little closer to the door, Ness realised she could never hope to hear anything through the solid oak. She walked to the window, pulling the heavy curtain aside a little. The sun was shining and the grounds looked beautiful; the views more than made up for the inside of the house, she thought, leaning in closer to the glass so she could get a better look through the pines of the distant purple hazed craggy hills. She'd have to take a long walk one day and explore them.

Hearing a sharp thud, Ness craned her head a little. Just to the left of the window the gardener was digging out a rotten tree stump. The guy was probably a total idiot but with a body like that, Ness mused, who cares. She watched his large hands expertly thrust the spade head into the soft ground. With each thrust of the spade his muscles bulged and beads of perspiration ran like rivulets down his sinewy back. With a final thrust of the spade, leaving it standing erect in the wet earth, he straightened up and stretched his arms above his head before striding off on long powerful legs. Ness leaned against the window frame, watching the gardener until he was out of sight she sighed. That is also something I should love to explore one day, she thought.

Turning back toward the study door Ness jumped. Ewan was standing directly behind her with a hungry look on his invidious pale face. He was suited as usual with his immaculate blonde hair in an Eton cut, clean shaven apart from his blonde tufty goatee and had spotlessly clean manicured nails he was, in appearance, flawless. Ness felt that there was something wholly unpleasant about the man, not just because he was so obviously a total letch. Which she supposed was a little hypocritical as she had spent the last five minutes lusting after the gardener, but she hated men that spoke to her breasts rather than her face and had once told a college lecturer that if he expected an answer he would have to ask her face not her tits.

"Ewan, I was admiring the view."

"So I see."

"I must take a walk in the hills one day, they look so beautiful and undisturbed."

"Yes, yes they are," he took a step closer to her. Ness stepped back and felt her backside up against the deep window sill. He was so close and she couldn't understand why, she normally so unshakable, felt so vulnerable He continued "they can also be dangerous places to explore by oneself, wild and untamed," he reached out and touched her hair, "such a pretty colour." A cough behind them made Ewan retract his fingers from Ness' hair and swivel round. Sir John stood in the open study doorway.

"It's 10am, Miss Gordon, I trust you are ready to start work."

Ness made her way round Ewan careful not to touch any part of him as she shimmied past. He stood solid, not budging an inch.

"Yes, of course Sir John, I was just admiring your grounds," Ness gratefully made her way into the study and sat down where he motioned to. She was surprised to find her hands shaking. She had no idea why the creep had provoked such a feeling of panic in her; she had been fine holding her own until he had wound a piece of hair around his long manicured finger and admired the colour. Those four little words sent a fear through Ness that she couldn't understand. Her heart was pounding in her chest and she felt nauseous.

For the next three hours Ness gratefully sank into work, she needed to get herself together and the routine of transcribing Sir John's dictaphone was doing the trick. Sir John himself was ensconced in some research, double checking dates and places. If Phil was hoping the book Ness was ghost writing would hold any juicy details of misgivings and wrong doings he would be sorely disappointed. So far it was all self-glorifying dribble it read like the hundred and one things that make me so wonderful by Sir John Woldarc.

The clock chimed one, "Lunch, Miss Gordon. You can finish that this afternoon."

"All done Sir John, if you have more notes for me I can do those. The sooner we can get started on the writing itself the better."

"Not in a rush to leave surely, Miss Gordon, you've only just arrived?"

"No of course not, it's just that I like to be busy and am looking forward to starting the writing properly. If you like I can help you with the research."

"That would be most helpful, thank you."

Lunch was as formidable as dinner the previous evening, served by a sour Agnes and seated opposite a slavering Ewan, Ness couldn't wait for the meal to end. Ness was glad to find that she had lost the feeling of inexplicable fear Ewan had stirred in her earlier, she found him repulsive but not terrifying and would certainly make sure that her bedroom door remained locked and never to be alone with him.

He had to be about her brother's age; forty, maybe slightly older. The gardener, on the other hand, she would cheerfully spend an hour or two alone in his company. She thought he had to be around thirty, maybe he could show her the hills and she could show him a few undulations of her own. Ness smiled crumbling the last of the cheese on her plate.

"What thought brings forth such an engaging smile, Ness?"

"I was hoping the sunshine would last so I can walk into the village this afternoon, have a look around," Ness silently prayed Ewan wouldn't offer to walk with her; even the sound of her name on his lips sounded lewd.

The afternoon's research didn't show Ness anything useful to her own purpose, Sir John didn't leave the room so there was no opportunity to do a little private snooping. Ness was thankful when Sir John announced she could knock off early as he had a couple of important business calls to make, business calls that would also engage Ewan fully, Ness happily noted.

The gardener who had been busy all the afternoon outside the study window packed up his tools into his barrow and headed off just as Ness was closing the study door. Maybe if she was quick she could catch up with him, ask if he would show her around when he knocked off work.

When Ness unlocked the door and walked into her room, instantly she knew someone had been in there. The faint sent of a strange fragrance and the contents of a drawer not as she had left them. Ness had learned a few tricks in her time, she had had too. A long habit of placing something folded up differently to the other contents of a packed drawer was an easy indication of someone fiddling. Everything was now folded the same and much too neatly. Her suitcase was around the wrong way under the bed and there was also the new addition of fresh

41

flowers sitting on the dresser and in the bathroom. Just in case they were caught in the act she supposed; gave them an excuse to be in there. The flowers, in Ness' opinion, showed the culprit to be Agnes: who else would bother?

Shoddy workmanship, Ness thought as she headed off down the drive way and turned left for the village.

The road was a secluded one and not one to be walked by the faint-hearted alone in the dark, the full hedgerows either side of the one car road and the forests of pine behind were picturesque on a sunny afternoon but night would bring menacing shadows and night time noises one only heard in the country.

Ness, remembering a country holiday she had when she had been a young girl, had thought the countryside to be a quiet place. She couldn't believe the blood-curdling yowls and shrieks.

Convinced they were going to be murdered in their beds, she had run into the lounge in terror only to be laughed at for her city ways by her brother and his friend. She had seen the funny side of things herself but not until safely snuggled on the couch, a mug of steaming hot chocolate in hand.

Miles away in a daydream of remembrance, Ness didn't hear the dark van come up behind her. It gave a toot and she dutifully stood on the grass verge to allow it to pass. It slowed to a walking pace to overtake her and just as it had passed and she had stepped back onto the road the back doors flew open and a tall dark haired man leapt out the back, grabbing Ness around the waist with one hand and pressing the other over her mouth. He heaved her roughly into the van. As she skidded into the back he leapt in after her pulling the doors closed and banging on the side. The van flew off and Ness, petrified mouth open to scream blue murder looked up at her assailant ready to fight tooth and claw and was shocked into silence.

Standing in front of her one hand on his hip the other supporting himself on the van roof, black hair tussled and a look of such rage she had never encountered on his face before was her brother.

Ness' tongue loosened from the roof of her mouth and anger replaced shock.

"Kalum! You fucking wanker... what the fuck do you think you're doing... you bastard!"

Ness made a move to stand, but Kalum was quicker and was suddenly towering over her and in a voice that scarcely contained his fury growled at her.

"Don't you move a muscle, don't speak!"

"I'll talk if I want to, you shit, how dare you..."

Ness's voice trailed off as Kalum grabbed her roughly by the arm and pulling her to her feet growled again.

"Last warning."

Ness swung her free arm back to slap him.

"Don't say I didn't warn you," he snarled as he twisted Ness around sat himself down on the wheel arch dragging her with him till she landed across his knee.

"I should have done this a long time ago," and holding Ness in place with one hand firmly by the back of her neck his strong legs pinning hers to his he brought his hand down hard on her rear. Ness cried out in shock and pain as his hand made contact with her backside echoing like a gunshot in the back of the van.

Ness tried to make a grab for any part of Kal that she could reach, which was nothing, she tried to push herself off his knee onto the van floor but he had her in a pincer grip and the more she struggled the tighter it got and the harder his hand slapped her backside.

"Stop it! You're hurting me," before the screamed words left her mouth she felt them to be an understatement of not only the pain but the humiliation she felt at his treatment. She couldn't understand what she had done. He had always submitted to her will, threatening punishments that never came to anything; one quiver of her bottom lip and she had whatever it was she wanted. This time the tears were real; hot angry tears of pain and lost dignity rolled down her cheeks.

Mark stole a look through the rear view mirror, he had seen his friend angry many a time but the cold fury on his face as he gave his sister about twenty years of back punishments was one he hadn't seen before. Then again, he reasoned, what he had seen and heard of Ness it wouldn't do her any harm. He stifled a laugh; god was she gonna be pissed off when she found out it was him driving, he hadn't missed her checking him out this morning. Hadn't missed the incident with Ewan in the hall either, or the look of sheer terror on her face. He hadn't been able to hear what he had said to Ness when he touched her hair but he had been ready to break it up with a well-aimed stone at the window and an excuse.

Now there was a creepy guy, specialised in torture – specifically the torture of females – and had a thing for red hair. His file read like a pornographic horror, he'd have to tell Kal about Ewan's unwanted attentions toward Ness. Mark stole another look in the mirror just as the final and hardest slap hit Ness's rump, he winced, ouch… not just now though.

The van drove down a leafy lane as dappled sunlight filtered through the trees and glinted off the windscreen. Mark pulled into a secluded pebble driveway and straight into a garage adjoining a Victorian whitewashed house. He jumped out the van, closing and locking the garage doors before thumping the side of the van.

"Okay," he called.

The double doors at the back of the van flew open and Kal jumped out pulling a sobbing but still kicking Ness with him. You had to admire the girl's stamina, thought Mark, as she aimed a kick at Kal's ankle, catching him unawares he swore and hoisted Ness over his shoulder continuing unabated.

Up a set of inner steps through the bright kitchen where Max was making a pot of tea and down some more steps into a large lounge. Kal dropped Ness unceremoniously onto a couch, she sprang straight back up, and he pushed her back down.

"I don't give a shit if your arse hurts to sit on Ness… sit down and shut up," he growled at her.

"I'd do as he says, dear," said Max as she deposited a tray of tea and biscuits on a side table.

Mark sat down near the door – the only escape route – grinning at Ness' shocked recognition as Max handed him a mug of tea and the biscuit tin.

Chapter Four

Whose Finger do you want on the Trigger?

When the World Situation is so Delicate?

– H Cudlipp, Publish and Be Damned.

"You! You're in this with him... did he pay you?" Ness looked at Mark full of scorn and derision. Her tone was arrogant; her words were intended to injure his pride. "I don't suppose gardeners earn much, so I hope he paid you well... when I sue your arse off you'll need it... I'll make sure you never get another job."

"Cup of tea, dear?" interjected Max, full of smiles and warmth.

"Piss off! No, I don't want your sodding tea," Ness swiped the offered mug out of Max's hand and it tumbled to the floor and smashed, the tea pooling at Kalum's feet.

Grabbing the front of her jacket, Kalum pulled Ness roughly to her feet. "Apologise now and clean the mess up! How dare you speak to Max in that way... you... rude... foul... little..." in silence he marched Ness into the kitchen and keeping a firm hold on her jacket, made her pick up a cloth and a dustpan and marched her back into the lounge. Max had picked up the large pieces of broken china.

"I thought they were a bit sharp to leave on the floor Kal," she nodded her head in Ness' direction.

"Yeah best not leave a lethal weapon lying around for me to make my escape with," Ness snarled at them.

"That's right dear," smiled Max heading off to the kitchen with the china. When she returned the floor was clean and Kalum, holding Ness firmly, shook her.

"Now apologise to Max," silence followed and Kal shook her once more "I said apologise... NOW!

"I'm very sorry for being so rude... being taken prisoner and assaulted always puts me in a temper."

Kalum raised his eyebrows. It was an apology of sorts. Mark, waving a chocolate biscuit in the air with a huge grin on his face said, "You know what... I can't remember when I last had such an entertaining afternoon, but Kal, mate," he paused to dunk his biscuit and with a mouth full carried on "time marches on and," he dunked another biscuit, "we haven't got to the good bit yet."

"I know the schedule Mark," Kal growled back.

"Just saying, mate."

"Sit down Ness," Kal moved Ness to the sofa so the backs of her legs were against the edge and roughly let go of her jacket. She fell into a sitting position wincing as she landed.

"We need to talk... more to the point I need to talk you need to listen... I don't expect to hear your voice or see your lips move until I give permission... clear?"

Ness motioned to her mouth and shrugging her shoulders as if asking a question. "Good, I'll take that as an agreement," Ness frowned. Standing in front of Ness with his large arms folded he continued.

"Firstly... It came to my attention yesterday that eight years ago. You," he poked her, "Instead of doing a degree at Portsmouth were in the employ of a dangerous criminal. You. Along with three other misguided idiots stole a virus from a locked lab. This virus was then put on the open market and sold to the highest bidder. The highest bidder was in this case the head of a terror organisation... who in turn sold it on to a communist regime where it could be used to its full potential. Threatening the very country you call home!" Kalum's voice was slowly rising his face was stony, cold. Fury emanated from every inch of him as he continued.

"Secondly. Two operatives were nearly killed retrieving the virus before it could be used," he paused, "it was going to be released in a primary school in central London for maximum impact... it would have course spread... it being an airborne virus with no antidote... thousands could have died because of your crass stupidity!

"Thirdly. Not content with the concept of mass murder, you continued on to petty thievery. How many people lost precious memories and personal items because of your idiocy and all to feed an amphetamine habit that started with you being seduced by a fucking terrorist! He leant into her face, she tried to move back. Want to see a picture of your dream man now Ness... It's an old photo taken five years ago when someone put a bullet in his skull," Kal whipped a photo out of a laptop bag that leant against the side table and tried to show Ness. Ness moved her face to the side not willing to look, Kalum grabbing her chin in one large hand forced her face around and with the other shoved the photo in front of her frightened downcast eyes.

"Look at it!" Ness slowly raised her eyes and focused on the print; she felt a little sick. It was his face all right: the eyes were open, empty and chilling. Half of his skull was missing and congealed blood and bits of brain were plastered down what was left of his face.

"Not so handsome now is he? Ness slowly shook her head and raising her white face to Kalum opened her mouth to speak.

"Shut it," he barked.

"Fourthly. You lied to me! You had to leave Portsmouth because you were kicked out... you were luckily given another place in London, helped to kick your drug habit and kept a close eye on ever since... and yes it was a friend of mum's that did that for you. He also kept you out of gaol. He is also my boss!" Kal paused, his chest heaving in indignation and rage, "He gave me your file to read yesterday because you are getting yourself involved where you shouldn't be involved... AGAIN!

"Fifthly. From now on you will listen to me! If you want to get out of this alive," he paused as her head shot up in shock. "No I don't mean I am going to kill you... I feel like it but, believe it or not there are others closer to you who will not hesitate to do so. You are in way over your head and I will tell you why and by whom in a moment but first I need to see your phone."

Kalum held his hand out expectantly waiting for Ness to hand it over. She hesitated; she didn't know what to do. When Kalum listed all those things she wasn't proud of, the way he said them made her feel like a criminal. A loser and, hell, she sounded like somebody she wouldn't want to meet, but that was just what she was, thought Ness, she was a thief and a liar but not anymore... she had put that all behind her... okay some of the tricks she had learnt still came in very useful but she hadn't touched drugs since. All of her contacts were on that phone... the files on Sir John... her own notes...

"HAND OVER YOUR FUCKIN PHONE NOW!" Kalum's booming shout broke Ness out of her reverie and knowing she had no choice shakily delved into her jacket pocket, retrieved the phone and handed it over.

"You won't get into it," she couldn't resist the quip.

"Watch me," he growled back.

Within minutes Kal was scrolling through Ness' phone. He found the files on Sir John and called to Mark, "Catch and read," Kal paced, throwing Ness looks of disgust while Mark read still seated by the door.

"I don't know where your crackpot editor got his info from Ness… but this is basically the worst type of bollocks I've seen in a long while… and believe me I've seen some bollocks in my time," he passed the phone back to Kalum who pressed delete files. Kalum flicked through the contacts, got Sir John's number up on Ness' phone and typed a text. 'APOLOGIES, WON'T BE BACK FOR DINNER. MET FRIEND IN VILLAGE STAYING THE NIGHT SEE YOU AT 10AM. N.'

Ness couldn't take any more. Kalum had unashamedly abused her, aired a past she wasn't proud of… in front of complete strangers. One of whom was Sir John's gardener, he had interfered with her work and was now not letting her leave. Her phone pinged and Kal opened the message. 'OK

WHERE ARE YOU STAYING AND I'LL SEND SOME THINGS DOWN FOR YOU.' Kal quickly typed. 'HILL HOUSE, DON'T PUT YOURSELF OUT I CAN BORROW. N.' He pressed send just as Ness, unable to sit and take it anymore, propelled herself forward and stood before Kal her rage almost matching his.

"YOU FUCKING WANKER! How... How dare you," she spluttered. "I'm leaving and you or your sodding lackeys can't stop me," she made a dash for the door, Mark was ready for her and grabbing her hard about her waist with one muscular arm said smiling,

"Oh no you don't sweetie, we haven't finished yet," Ness tried to kick and force Mark's arm off her with her hands he just laughed. "Must be all that gardening... builds your muscles... where do you want her Kal?"

"Bathroom. I'm right behind you."

Mark easily tipped Ness over his shoulder and carried her up to the bathroom, Max busied herself loading the dishwasher and sat down to read a magazine in a lounge chair by the window where she had a good view of the driveway. She was curled up looking cosy as if she had been there for hours, when Kal made to follow Mark and Ness up to the bathroom. Ness was causing Mark as much aggravation as possible and had bitten his hand as he tried to cover her mouth.

"You going to be all right, Max?"

"Sure Kal, believe me I'll scream if I need you."

Kal had just entered the bathroom and shot the bolt through when there was a knock at the front door. Turning the bathroom radio on and the shower on full he motioned to Mark to bring Ness to him and whispering in her ear he said "If you make one sound… one whisper… your pants are coming down this time… in front of him… and believe me if you thought it hurt before…" he left the sentence open.

Mark grinned and whispered, "I don't mind… really… if you need to… let it out… a squeak will do it for him… man of his word is Kal," Ness fell silent. The murmur of voices below drifted up to them, after about five minutes they heard Max showing someone out asking if they were sure they wouldn't like a cup of tea; she was sure Ness wouldn't be long. The reply being a negative one the door closed. Max settled back into her chair and resumed reading the magazine. The car waited outside for a couple of minutes before heading off down the drive. Ten minutes elapsed before Kalum deemed it safe to unlock the door.

He turned around and looked in astonishment at Mark. Trickles of blood were slowly running down his knuckles.

"You bit him? Right! Don't say you weren't warned," as he made a move toward Ness, her eyes widened in alarm. He stopped just as he was reaching out for her and laughed. "Sure thing mate," Ness couldn't see Mark motioning to Kal behind her, but he jerked his head toward the shower and grinned.

Kal flicked the shower onto cold as Mark picked Ness up easily from behind and before she understood what was happening she found herself sat in the bottom of the bath. Icy cold water cascading down over her. She flailed in the slippery bath as Mark's strong hand was pressed firmly to the top of her head.

Kal laughed. "I'll go and get her some dry clothes… looks like you got it under control."

Mark waited until he heard Kal thumping downstairs then lent a little in toward Ness and spoke in a low grainy voice.

"One of us would have to take a cold shower… I chose you… bite me again and take the consequences."

Kal entered the bathroom with an arm full of dry clothes for Ness. "I'll leave you to it mate," and winking wickedly at a wide eyed Ness, Mark turned the shower off and left.

It was half an hour later that, blushing from embarrassment, Ness re-emerged in the lounge with Kal's hand firmly on her shoulder. The indignity of being forced to get dried and dressed behind the large towel her brother was holding had forced Ness into silence.

Mortified, she couldn't meet Mark's eye and gratefully received the hot coffee Max held out to her. She needed a smoke; surely he wouldn't stop her from doing that? She cleared her throat.

"I need a cigarette."

"No you don't, you want one, and you don't need one."

"Kal. Please can I have a cigarette... I'll go outside and smoke it," Ness was almost begging. Max interrupted.

"You can smoke in the kitchen... I was going to have one anyway, come on."

Kal motioned to Mark to go with them, he stood leaning nonchalantly against the kitchen dresser, arms folded, watching Ness like a hawk while she chain smoked two cigarettes.

"You should consider giving up, smoking's a bad habit."

"Go to hell."

"Naw... been there didn't like it... what we having for dinner, Max?"

"Chinese. I've ordered a takeout, it should be here at seven," Max had finished her own cigarette and was loading Ness' clothes into the washer. She dropped Ness' pants; Mark grinned cheekily "Looks like I've seen them anyway."

Ness flamed beetroot as Max took a swipe at Mark with a teatowel.

Kal walked through, "Come on. Lots to get through," he looked at his sister with veiled concern "It's going to be a long night and if we want any sleep we need to start now."

Running his hand through his thick black hair Kal motioned for Ness to go in front. He was not looking forward to this... at all... he had no idea of how Ness would react... but she sure as hell needed to know the truth... needed to know what she was dealing with...needed to know what the sadistic bastard was capable of... how much danger she was in if she stayed... hell she couldn't stay... he would have to make sure she understood... where to begin and how far to go... did she need to know what happened to their mum... he thought not just yet... he had enough evidence to put in front of her of the other poor bitches he had mutilated, tortured to death... some just for kicks when he was bored... the guy had perfected the art of taking someone to the point of death and allowing them as much recovery time as needed to start the whole process over again... he filmed it, presumably so he could study his technique... improve on his skills. Kal snorted with derision. Ness thought Sir John was the baddy... he was in it up to his aristocratic armpits... they had enough evidence of that... thought he was head honcho... best buds with не мне... no Sir John wasn't the problem... just an overinflated ego with the right connections and a bulging bank balance... to be used and hung out to dry like a lamb to the slaughter when his worth had been spent.

Worrying too, were the files Phil sent through to Ness. Complete bollocks was an understatement. There was enough trumped up evidence there to do one of two things. If не мне's plans went awry all blame would lay squarely at Sir John's door... no other evidence of involvement would exist... on the other hand if things went well they would need Sir John... someone of money and influence; a foot in the door of the power house... If the Scottish independence vote had been successful they would already be half way there... Britain would be divided and the door would be well and truly open... the chief was right about the masses... they bleated and they followed but who or where to, they didn't understand... until it was too late... parties with a hidden agenda from the mother land had to be stopped... when would people learn... it's not like it hadn't been attempted before... history... why did people not pay attention to history?

The curtains had been drawn in the lounge as the heavens opened. The sound of rain hammering onto the drive was comforting as they sat in the cosy glow of the fire Mark had lit; the evening had turned chilly as the rain swept the country side in great sheets and the wind gushed through the pines howling as it battered the outside of the house.

Kal sat opposite Ness. "I need you to pay attention to what I am going to tell you," he paused and, sitting an ashtray at her side, carried on ignoring the surprised look on her face. "Questions can be asked when I say and not before... it is important I am not interrupted... it is also important you are clear on all I am about to tell you... Understood?"

"Over and out," Ness saluted. He chose to ignore her sass.

"We," he made a sweeping gesture across the room, "work for the intelligence services. I have been employed by the organisation for approximately twenty years.

"You have got yourself mixed up in yet another operation to bring Britain and the free world to her knees. Led by people who still deem America as the number one enemy and Britain as number two.

Your immediate boss Sir John is up to his eyeballs in it... but his main crimes are of greed, vanity and stupidity... he is not the man to be worried about... не мне is. Sir John's Soviet puppeteer is a murderous treacherous bastard who kills people off in lots of ingenious ways if they cross him. He is dangerous, desperate for glory and is doing all he can to return Russia to the good old days of the USSR. не мне is not our friend or ally. His heart always has been and always will be KGB. They're now called FSB, but it's the same organisation, same principles, same goals, with the old KGB in its ranks.

The cold war is not over... spying on western countries peeked cold war levels a decade ago and continues to rise... Snowden has armed Moscow and its allies with ammo designed to bring about the downfall of Britain's and America's intelligence communities. He ran his hand through his hair and sighed. large numbers of the general public have expedited his efforts by doing exactly what they were intended to do... mass protest to shut down surveillance... which also opens the door to major terror organisations... follow me so far?"

Ness nodded, silently lighting up a cigarette. She looked at her brother in a whole new light... would make one hell of an exclusive... fuck Phil, this was her story. If she was in on the action then she'd have all the information at her finger tips... by the time Kalum read the headline she'd be sunning herself on a distant shore... because he sure as hell wouldn't agree to an interview.

"Don't misunderstand me, Sir John is not a nice guy, but compared to the bastard he takes his orders from he's a pussycat. His chief in the UK is a narcissistic psychopath. Tortures his victims to death usually for his own gratification but his technique comes in handy when they want someone to talk. His objectives are female... it's his speciality. Picks up homeless girls; they're easy targets especially if they have an addiction. He has money and offers to spend it on them for a small service, they go willingly without a fuss. Young runaways: he promises them a hot meal and a bed for the night, says he'll help them, does a convincing gay act, they feel safe. These girls are already missing and usually no one's looking for them. Videos his work, plays it back for pleasure and to advance his technique.

We managed to obtain a copy of one... it's the foulest thing I have ever seen and Ness, believe me, I have seen some nauseating stuff in my time. As Mark puts it they look like a very twisted pornographic horror," the doorbell rang.

Mark pushed himself up from the armchair silently and Kal whispered to Ness, "We can't be seen, they may still be watching. Can I trust you or do I have to take you with us?"

Ness shook her head, "You have my undivided attention, I am riveted and bloody starving," Once the men were in the kitchen Max opened the door for the takeaway delivery.

From their position behind the kitchen door Max's light easy voice drifted through, "Oh you poor boy, you're soaked through! I would feel guilty if I wasn't so hungry. Oh dear, I think I've over-ordered... again. Looks like dinner tomorrow night taken care of too," she laughed as she pressed a fiver into the teenager's outstretched grateful soggy hand.

The soft glow of the wall lamps against the old whitewashed kitchen walls made a chilly atmosphere warm. The curtains were closed against the still wailing wind and the rain lashed against the old wooden frames rattling the glass secured within them.

They ate in silence. Mark and Kalum wolfing their food down in great forkfuls, Max was reading the local paper while Ness after a few mouthfuls began to toy with her noodles as she thought up various eye catching headlines for her exclusive. She imagined her by line nestled next to the earth shattering headline in bold type. 'JOURNALIST POLLUTES HE MEHЯ PLOT TO BATTER BRITAIN' By Ness Gordon.

"Thought of a good headline?" Mark enquired. Ness was now thinking up ways to get some photos to accompany her piece, entirely lost in her reverie she answered honestly with a small laugh. "Yeah, but how am I go... Shit!" Her fork clattered onto the table, her hand covered her mouth as she gaped at Mark. He grinned and waving his fork in Kalum's direction said "You owe me a tenner," before reloading it with noodles and winking roguishly at Ness.

Kalum was silent. His eyes narrowing and pushing the empty Chinese cartons away from him he leant forward, his arms on the table top. Ness gulped nervously and through Kalum's silence felt forced to speak. "You never said I couldn't have the exclusive... it's my job... It's like saying to you watch the bad guys but don't catch them," Mark finally finished with his meal wiped his hand across his mouth and said, "Like I've been doing for the past year you mean."

His narrowed eyes still on his sister, Kalum decided it was time to move on. There was no way she would be writing about this, he'd see to that.

"Listen up... this man is ready to play again. He hasn't satisfied his blood lust for a while; his last victim in Britain was over a year ago... he was in Russia six months ago for three days. We can only guess at what he was doing.

"His code name is FLAKE, so called for his alabaster skin and snow-white hair. He is without a doubt one of the most evil bastards to walk the earth... you know him as Ewan."

Chapter Five

But not so odd

As those who choose

A Jewish God,

But spurn the Jews.

– *Cecil Browne*

Ewan walked through the great double doors and stood dripping on the polished tile floor peeling off his wet coat and dropping it at his feet. He wore a cruel and joyful smirk.

"I know you're there, Agnes, watching from the shadows as usual," his voice: silky mocking happy, was enough to make her thin bony shoulders shudder. She was standing just behind the old baize door that led from the kitchens peering through the dim hall light at his profile. He had been worried when they had received Ness' message still unsure as to the girl's true intentions. Was she a plant or just unfortunate in her choice of employment?

His thinly veiled anticipation suggested the latter. The girl's story of staying with a friend must have checked out; he had been through her belongings on the first night and again when she left for the village. There was nothing to suggest any sinister motive on her part, no hidden agendas or outside influence. He called again. She walked slowly out of her hiding place, determined to show only her disgust of him and none of the fear that coursed through her body.

"Ah… there you are," his tone was one of speaking to a small child that was enjoying a game of hide and seek.

Gusting winds forced the heavy unlatched door open just as she made her way forward the gale howled around him, blowing his sleek white hair into a halo around his alabaster face, wearing its joyful mask. The anticipation of cruelty to come. He looked like the angel of death; his long fingers made shadows like marble talons across the hall floor in the grey light, the talons to snare his prey pointed to his coat on the floor.

"I'll be in the cellar and I don't wish to be disturbed," Agnes nodded, moving around him to close the heavy doors. Ewan moved off to the stairs that led down to the large cellar humming as he went.

Agnes, holding the sodden coat, shivered. She had seen Ewan's private cellar, hidden neatly behind Sir

John's large store of wine and whiskey. By walking through a small wooden door that was virtually hidden behind a large book case standing from floor to cobwebbed ceiling. That opened out to reveal a small dingy corridor a large heavy hessian curtain hung on the Wall at the end. Pulling the dirty hessian aside revealed a shining steel door: the only way in or out was to know the key code.

"I know what you do in your cellar and I've seen your revolting trophy case," Agnes whispered after him so only she could hear," it was something she would never forget. That dreadful night. Hearing a car pull up she had rushed to her usual place at the baize door and seen Ewan walk in with a young woman, she was dressed poorly and obviously drunk, he was holding her up. She was laughing. Her carrot red hair pulled into a high pony tail... she had looked very young. He had shushed her and whispered something into her ear that made her blush to the very roots of her red fringe.

Agnes had waited a while then followed them down to the cellar; to fetch up a bottle of scotch for medicinal purposes, she had a slight sniffle and why shouldn't she go into her own cellar? Once she had picked out a bottle Agnes opened the small door and made her way down the corridor, the steel doors were fractionally ajar the blood-curdling scream that suddenly thrust itself through the gap closely followed by another and another made her freeze in her tracks, then that voice...

"Such a pretty colour...red," a girl's violent sobs begging for mercy for him to stop before the screaming started again.

She had run as she had never run before straight to her room locking herself in and with an unsteady hand poured a large tumbler of whiskey. She had gone back the next day, the compelling urge to see what was behind that door couldn't be denied... it had been fowl. She had also seen what was hanging in neat rows in a glass cabinet... she ran for the outside for the clean untainted air and just made it to the front doors before she vomited. Spending that day and the next in her room with a 'stomach bug'. Agnes didn't think she could face the monster again... but she had... she had been given no choice.

Now he had chosen a new victim. When the girl arrived with her long striking red hair Agnes had known. Even before she had seen the hungry look of anticipation on his sickening face, she had known how Ness' life would end... screaming in agonies that couldn't be imagined... locked in the cellar. Agnes knew too well that neither she nor John could ever speak out against it; that they were incriminated and Moscow would not hesitate to resort to the usual technique of blackmail to ensure their silence... blackmail that had been resorted to once already... that's why she was still here. Agnes clucked her tongue in a noise of disgust... John was an idiot... stupid inflated bigot... he honestly believed the promise made to him in Moscow.

Agnes smiled maliciously as she finished sponging the worst of the rain off of Ewan's coat. Things could change...tables can be turned... if Ewan were discovered... if he was caught and ousted for his sick crimes then Moscow would disown him and не мне would order his death... a death that would be untraceable to не мне and Moscow... just like all the others that had spoken out or embarrassed the party... She allowed herself a small giggle before covering her mouth... if an oligarch's tax evasion in Britain earned him a bullet through the head what would be не мне instruction for mass murder... overlooking those crimes carried out in Moscow on his command of course. God knows she had tried to persuade John to get rid of Ness as soon as she had seen her, tried to make the girl feel so uncomfortable that she would leave on her own accord... hell, she must have the skin of a rhinoceros... Ewan needed to be caught in the act with the evidence of his crimes for all to see and hopefully the girl could be saved... no one deserved to die like that.

Agnes, carrying the coat to the small laundry room off the kitchen, wondered just how it was going to be managed without incriminating herself. Making her way upstairs she stopped at Ness's open bedroom door. Ewan, flush with expectation, was busy hiding the first of the small video cameras, he had three with him and intended to put one in the bathroom, one in the dresser and one above the bed.

"I thought you were in the cellar not to be disturbed," her disgust barely concealed.

"I was," he answered briskly "and I will be again as soon I've finished with this... just a little project of mine," he turned toward her curling his lip maliciously, "nothing for you to concern yourself with," and he waved her on.

Grateful to reach the sanctuary of her rooms Agnes locked and bolted the door, she'd run herself a nice hot bath... get rid of the tainted feeling caused by the memories he had stirred in her.

Ewan watched Agnes scurry down the corridor. He thought her stupid... ugly and so deathly dull. He enjoyed mocking her, it relieved his boredom.

Turning back to the task in hand his face lit up... he had never been given the opportunity to do anything like this before, he could really get under her skin, get to know her better... every naked inch of her... decide what he was going to do first... where to make that first all-important incision. He wanted to see all of her, from every angle, every crease and join... her breasts had looked full and firm under the tight fitting dress she had worn that night at dinner and it had accentuated her delightfully rounded bottom... he thought unclothed it would be a perfect heart shape and wondered if she masturbated... he hoped so, to catch a glimpse of her gaping open eager quim as her fingers frantically rubbed and tweaked her clit before his very eyes was something he had never seen before. It would be like she was performing for him and he could play it back to her as he worked on her cunt... now that would be a thrill... and the end film would be entrancing... a true masterpiece.

When the last camera was installed he switched them on with the remote in his pocket and lay on her bed, his long thin legs bent knees together, he let them relax and fall. Rubbing his crotch he beamed up at the camera... that last one had been so long ago. She was so obviously inexperienced. He tutted crossly as if it had been the girl's fault she could not withstand the pain he had inflicted on her. He had made no improvements of his skill and she hadn't lasted long at all... It was no fun if you couldn't see the fear in their eyes, so unsatisfying. But this one. Oh, oh! She held promise... yes he was going to enjoy this one... take his time... planning... watching... waiting. Smiling into his camera he gave a little wave and hid a coquettish titter behind his creamy white hand. Before he left the room he smoothed the sheets and checking all was as he found it made his way happily back to the cellar. He couldn't wait to turn on his laptop.

Sir John was in the cellar dusting the cobwebs off a bottle of 1968 Merlot, swaying slightly he whistled an old fashioned ditty. Turning as Ewan came up behind him, "Ah Ewan... care to join? He held the bottle aloft like a trophy.

"Not tonight...I have a little project I'm working on," he carried on walking.

"Ewan!" turning at John's sharp tone he stopped and raised a quizzical eyebrow.

70

"I hope your plans do not involve Miss Gordon... I don't want her harmed, Ewan... if needs be I'll..." he left the sentence unsaid as Ewan moved towards him.

"I have my work to do just as you have yours... I suggest we don't interfere with each other's," he stalked off around Sir John and was just about to disappear behind the bookcase.

"Ewan! I'll have to interfere if I have to bury another poor bitch in my bloody wood, this isn't just about you... remember we have a purpose... an important job to do... if you get caught," John gulped, the thought was not a pleasant one. The media interest alone would ruin him and what would Moscow say? He'd be to blame for letting Ewan get careless... years of planning down the drain and what would happen to him... he wouldn't be allowed to just carry on... he'd be hung out to dry... prison if the British authorities got to him first and death if they didn't... a suicide... or an accidental shooting whilst cleaning his shotgun. That was the usual way... he may be summoned to Moscow if he wasn't in custody here... summoned to his death... no, he thought not... he'd die by the не мне long arm here on his own estate with no witnesses and no one would be brought to justice for his death.

"Leave the girl alone Ewan. Why don't you go away for a few days, eh? Play your sick game away from here... where it's safe," and if you get caught, he thought, it can't come back on me.

Ewan stopped in his tracks and with his head to one side considered Sir John. He wondered silently if he could make her last a few days... two maybe... it would obviously have to be here, all his tools were here... but no one else needed to know he was here... if he planned it well... thought it all through. He smiled at John.

"I'll think about it John... and I promise you I will not make a move on Ness whilst she is in your employ. How about that?"

John smiled with relief, "Thank you Ewan, I knew you'd understand... good man. Good man!"

He started up his ditty again and headed for the upstairs. Ewan watched him leave before ducking behind the book case and heading down the small concealed corridor.

Typing in the combination. The date that Great Britain would fall... that glorious day when she would legally and stupidly in the name of democracy open her doors wide to the one and true leader... the day the proletarians, waving their idiot banners would willingly enter Britain into the chaos of a darkening Europe, a Europe that would be warring within itself... This time they would succeed, without a united Britain to stand against them to rally and unite... then... then he could have his pick. No need to sneak around in the dark picking up the lost and the rejected. His lip curled into a sneer, Bah... stupid worthless whores... they stank of booze and had the needy selfish grasp of the addict... he was sick of the stink of them... but soon... very soon all that would change.

They had so many of their own on the inside, in every position of influence and power. The rich, the famous, the policy makers and the peacekeepers... and of course the rising rabble, a few well-placed boys and young men all wiling to follow a cause to their death if required... and for most of them it would be compulsory... they just didn't realise it yet... by the time they did it would be too late... nowhere for them to run, no one to protect and fight for them.

He entered his den and with an eager anticipation checked his camera angle on his laptop, playing back himself in Ness' room. He was happy. Crossing to a curtained cabinet and pulling the curtains aside he smiled lovingly at the contents all neatly on display behind the glass.

Where there was greed and corruption they infiltrated... it was so easy... Britain had become a gluttonous nation full of materialistic self-interested people... all ready to follow whomever promised them more... more of what didn't matter.

Yes. Hers would be the pinnacle of his collection. His long immaculate fingers stroked the glass, caressing the protective covering of his life work. One day, it would be on display in his own private office... he would have to get another two or possibly three cabinets... he could line his walls as others line theirs with bookcases... no need to hide them... not then.

Turning around, Ewan viewed the room with qualified criticism. The gleaming stainless steel workbenches with the drawers neatly concealed in the front of each. He pulled opened one drawer at a time inspecting his tools, taking each knife out and examining it closely, checking the edges against his thumb for sharpness, then the scalpels, the butchers' hooks, the saws and the clamps. All shiny and as sharp as the day he last used them. Satisfied, he turned his attention to the main feature of the room.

A large stainless steel autopsy table with the additions of metal leg stirrups and leather body straps set at varying stages along both sides sat atop a two tiered plinths. The fluorescent lighting that shone from directly above hit the steal and sent rainbows around the stark white bright walls. Above the table coiled against the ceiling like a vast metal cobra was a pulley system of his own making; he could attach any part of the chain to the subject's holding straps and with a small pull manoeuvre any part of them into the position of his choice. Around the coiled pulley was a thick metal strip. Inlaid into the strip were various small cameras so he could catch every possible angle, the main camera sat opposite the table along with extra lighting if needed.

To each side of the table was a small gleaming steel table on wheels. Each had on the top of its shiny surface glass containers of various sizes, a box of latex gloves sat next to them.

On the opposite wall was a large double sink. On the drainer next to it was a long length of hose complete with tap attachments. Ewan nodded with satisfaction, everything was ready, he only had to watch and wait... that would give him some time to think of some new exciting ways to prolong Ness' time on his table... he'd treat himself right now... why not? He flicked off the luminous bright lights and crossed to the far side of the room stopping by his desk. He opened a drawer and selecting a DVD; he sunk it into the player and turned on the TV. He was always careful to use the TV and not the laptop when entertaining himself; you never knew who could be watching... no point in giving Moscow ammunition to blackmail him with.

Very slowly. Deliberately. He undressed; folding up each garment neatly and setting them aside. He crossed the room naked and stopping at the cabinet opened the glass doors, taking his time, finger on chin in deliberation he carefully selected a treasure from within. Cradling it between his hands he walked to his desk and pressing play sat in the chair. Long legs wide apart, his penis was erect and hard as the girl on the screen began to scream.

Placing his treasure on his head and flattening the long auburn curls until they sat as naturally on his head as if his own hair, he stroked the tresses in one long movement, caressing his nipples with his thumbs as he passed them and continued downwards until he held his penis in one cold white hand. With the other he gradually coiled a strand of red curls around his finger and raised it to his mouth to gently kiss the dead locks.

The girl on the screen screamed in agony, begging her torturer to stop. He was positioned between her outstretched thighs, only his back visible between her shackled ankles, his head leaning in close to her vulva, both invisible skilled and dreadful hands busy in their art. Her eyes widened with shock as she tried to arch her back against the strong leather thong bound tight around her waist; trying in hopelessness to move away from those cruel hands wielding their tools of horror. Her arms outstretched, equally bound, her hands balled into fists against the pain. The screams turned into one long anguished shriek at the realisation that there would be no mercy and the help she begged for so desperately would never be forthcoming.

Ewan, smiling at the screen, passionately kissed the hair between his fingers and began to masturbate.

Chapter Six

They who can give up essential liberty to purchase a little temporary safety deserve neither liberty nor safety.

– Benjamin Franklin

Ness woke early. The summer sun was sending rays of bright gold through the bedroom curtains; the stream of light danced on the walls and across the bed cover. Rolling over she checked the time on her wristwatch…6am. Ness yawned; it had been a long night.

Pushing back the bed cover she swung her legs over the side of the bed and sat for a moment listening to the silence, thinking about the previous night.

Kalum had been insistent that she leave Woldarc House today and get on the first train back to Oxford; she of course had no intention of doing so and had told him that if he thought he could order her around he was mistaken. She had a job to do, nothing was going to stop her from doing her job and she most certainly didn't need his permission. Kalum had stridden around the kitchen table and without a word had pulled Ness to her feet and with a grip of iron silently marched her into the lounge. Mark had followed and when he saw that Kalum was loading a memory stick into the television he interrupted.

"Er Kal mate," there was no answer. Unperturbed Mark continued. "We agreed Kal, that watching that may prove more destructive than helpful," he nodded in Ness's direction.

This time Kalum answered his voice held an emotion more than anger and Ness couldn't work out what it was. "She's not going to be watching... just listening," he led Ness over to the sofa and sat her down. Mark and himself on either side, he tied a folded tea towel around Ness's eyes and pressed play.

Ness shuddered at the memory, she had been made to sit for what felt like hours listening to a girl's screams of despair and agonising pleas for help, for mercy, for mummy, sobbed that she was sorry she had run away. The girl's breathing was harsh and laboured; Ness couldn't begin to imagine what was being done to cause such agonies but that the girl was in severe pain and distress was plain to hear. The last was the worst: a high pitched wailing that ended in a gurgled sob and then silence.

Ness felt Kalum move next to her and the next moment her blindfold was wiped off and she was staring at a still screen; Ewan's manic face frozen in ecstasy, his mouth open, he was covered in blood and just behind him she could see a pair of limp feet held tight in stirrups. Kalum, standing next to the television, switched it off and stood staring down at Ness's pale wide eyed face.

It was a while before anyone spoke. Kalum eventually broke the silence.

Pointing at the now black screen, he said "That is the first reason why you will not be going back... you have possibly... no... definitely been marked as his next victim," he paused, studying her face, hoping what she had just seen and heard wouldn't awaken memories... memories from a six year old mind so horrific she had blanked them out. "The second reason is much more complicated... I have told you a little about it already but can't give you much more... you just have to trust me and for once in your life do as I say."

Ness had nodded silently and asked to be shown to her bed. There was no point in arguing further. She had no intention of doing as Kalum had asked, regardless of what she had just heard and seen.

Now in the bright morning sun, Ness reminded herself that the girl on the screen would never enjoy a summer morning and the only way to help her now was to bring the bastard to justice and get the story... she had to return to the house... carry on with the job and she would have to pull herself together and be professional. Dressing noiselessly and creeping to the

79

bedroom door, as quietly as possible she began to turn the handle a little at a time. When the knob was fully turned she pulled the door... nothing happened. She tried again a little harder. The bastard had locked the fucking door. Ness fumed and looked around for another escape route her eye fell on the window.

It didn't look a huge drop. The porch was just under the bedroom window and to the side of the porch was a bench. She could see the edge of the worn wood; it meant she could lower herself in three stages. Ness sat on the ledge and wondered if she could get away with it. With single-minded tenacity she nodded and hanging her handbag around her neck and shoulder, lowered one leg over then the other and sucking in a big breath of air she began to climb down.

As quietly as she could, Ness lowered herself onto a small wooden bench that sat on one side of the porch. Old flower pots stood on each end. Her boot tapped the side of one as she tried to position her weight equally between them. Ness stood stock-still both hands still holding onto the edge of the porch, heart pounding as the pot swayed. If it fell onto the pavers beneath the game was up and she didn't want to think of Kalum's reaction if he found her clinging to the side of the house. No excuse would cover it, he would probably have her locked up.

The pot settled back onto its base and Ness let out the breath she was holding. Gradually she inched herself onto the pavers palms against the wall for support as she let down each foot. At last she was standing on solid ground listening to the silence that still surrounded the early morning.

Ness inched her way around the side of the house, aiming for the thick hedgerow that stood around the borders, if she could reach the hedgerow and duck through then she would be able to walk over the fields that lay behind and enter Woldarc House through the wood that lay beyond the fields of waving Barley. Bending down low with her back to the wall Ness, crablike, made her way along the side of the house. The lounge curtains were closed but Ness couldn't be sure if anyone else was up and didn't want to risk her shadow showing through the material.

By the time Ness had made it to the dense green hedge and struggled through the thicket she was hot, grubby and had bits of twig and leaves stuck in her hair. Making her way on all fours till she reached a hollow in the ground and judging she was far enough away from the house to be spotted from any windows. Ness sat and scrabbled in her handbag for a cigarette. Lighting it she took an appreciative drag carefully blowing the smoke out and away from her, wishing she had a coffee to go with it. Checking her watch, she noted with some surprise that the whole episode had taken under an hour – it had felt like a lot longer. Feeling around inside her bag for her mobile she realised, just as his shout bellowed like a newly castrated bull ricocheted across the field, Kalum still had her phone.

Quickly stubbing out her cigarette, she was undecided. Run for it or stay put? Stay put. She'd never out run him. Her heart hammering in her chest she clutched her bag close to her and sat stock-still hardly daring to breath.

"Where the fuck are you Ness... you fucking irresponsible little bitch... when I get my hands on you... you are so gonna wish you'd followed my orders," feeling about in his jeans pocket for his mobile he whipped it out and pressed in a number.

"She's gone... through the bedroom window... heading your way."

"Shit! I thought she was to ready and willing to agree with you last night... gave in too easy... from what I've seen of her so far, not her style at all."

"Tell me something I don't know Mark... when I get hold of her..."

"Should have taken up watch in her room like I said, I did volunteer."

"Shut it Mark! You have to stop her... she has to know who Max and I are supposed to be... Shit... shit... SHIT!" Ness could hear Kalum kicking hard at the gravel as he swore.

"You calling this one in? He wants to be kept informed of your erm... progress."

"Not yet."

"Fair enough… If she's gone across the fields she'll come out at the woods… if she went out the front she'll be coming up the drive… what you want me to do with her when I get her."

"I don't care what you do with her just make sure she understands what's at stake if she blows our cover… and tell her… tell her… I'll be seeing her soon. And Mark?"

"Yes, mate."

"Keep her safe," Kalum rang off walking back into the house calling himself every type of bloody fool… a fool for believing that Ness would do as she was ordered… a fool for falling for the oldest trick in the book… when he got hold of her he was going to wring her bloody obstinate neck.

Throwing himself into a kitchen chair he glowered at Max as she set a steaming mug of coffee in front of him. She sat down opposite him with her own mug, ignoring his scowl.

"You know what?" she asked him

"What?"

"Well, firstly if you continue to look at me like it's my fault your sister is more like you than you care to admit… I will hurt you… severely," she took a sip of coffee watching him over the top of the mug.

"Secondly, Ness managed to exit this house without any of us knowing until she was well away… not an easy thing to achieve," Kalum still angry moved forward in his seat and opened his mouth to disagree, Max held her hand up to silence him.

"Thirdly, as you pointed out to her she has been in… erm… let's say difficult situations before and whether you like it or not has learnt a thing or two about survival.

"Fourthly, Mark will get to her before she can do any damage.

"Fifthly, You still have her phone… which not only gives you an opportunity to get her back here… or you up there… but also opens up the possibilities of knowing exactly where she is and who is calling her and vice versa.

"Lastly… and I know you don't like it… Ness is up to her neck in this… Flake has her marked… she could be helpful… as long as we have her back at all times… she should be safe," Max watched Kalum's face closely he hadn't liked what she was telling him. His dark eyes were almost black; a sure sign of his fury. Silence sat heavy in the kitchen, the only sound apart from Kalum's breathing was the ticking of the kitchen clock, they stared at each other from opposite ends of the table. Max didn't lower her eyes, lit a cigarette and took another sip of coffee. She had known Kalum for twenty years had been through hell with him and come out the other side… changed… they both were… but whole… she knew her words had hit home and that he was struggling with himself at this moment and that he would see reason before she had finished her coffee.

Leaning back in his chair he sighed, picked up his coffee, took a large gulp, set down the cup and then spoke.

"You are as always right, Max... Mark will catch her and fill her in... we can watch her and we can, after a few minor adjustments... arrange for her to collect her phone... I don't like it, Max... not one little bit... we pull her out quickly if we need to... and that will be my call... agreed?"

"Agreed," Max smiled at him, pouring more coffee into their cups.

Ness stayed hidden until she heard her brother go inside. Inching slowly on all fours she made her way along the hedgerow; the ground was wet and muddy from last night's storm. A wood pigeon flew out of the hedge, cooing angrily at her she ducked to avoid it slipping into a deep muddy puddle. Ness swore; hoisting her bag further up her back she pulled herself up the other side of the hole. Looking up and seeing the edge of the wood a few metres away Ness stood up and ran for the cover of the thick pine. Kalum stood in Ness' room. He was nailing the sash windows firmly closed... if he had to bring her back... correction... when he brought her back he didn't want to risk her leaving the same way. Trying the window and satisfied it wouldn't budge a figure in the distance caught his eye.

Smiling he pulled his mobile out of his pocket and dialled.

"She's heading into the woods now... call me when you've got her."

Ness ran until she judged she was deep enough in and slid down the trunk of the nearest pine, gasping for breath and fumbling in her bag she pulled out her cigarettes and lit one up. Her mouth was dry – she thought longingly of the coffee pot in her room and promised herself a massive pot full of steaming hot coffee as soon as she got back. Ness looked down at herself; her hands were covered in mud and clumps of wet earth, leaves and bits of twig were sticking to her, she'd also need a shower and a change of clothes.

Lighting up another cigarette and taking a deep drag Ness wondered how she was going to get back in to the house without being noticed; the state she was in would take some explaining. Ah well, she would come to that if needed, she was good at thinking up excuses on the cuff. Finishing her cigarette she pushed herself up, brushed her hands down her jeans and looked around. Which direction should she go in? She shrugged her shoulders and made roughly for the way she thought the house was.

Mark found Ness before she had finished her second smoke. Watching from the shadows he started off when she did; soundless and stealthy he choose his moment to spring.

Ness stopped by a large thickset tree. It was difficult to judge where she was in the gloom. Squinting into the distance she could just make out red brick and was about to move off when a large rough hand pressed itself over her mouth and a thick muscled arm drew tightly around her waist pinning her arms at her sides and pulled her backwards into a hard sculpted chest.

Mark picked Ness up as he was holding her and walked off without uttering a sound. He knew she was scared; he could feel her pulse thumping fast in her neck, serve her bloody right too. Reaching the small brick hut he kicked open the door and with one long leg closed it the same way and, still silent, dumped her face down on the camp bed with his knee in the small of her back. He pulled her hands around and tied them securely behind her. He then did the same to her ankles before stuffing a wad of cotton into her mouth and pulling a bandana out of his back pocket, he put it around her mouth and tied it neatly and tightly at the back of her head.

The whole operation had taken just minutes. Ness hadn't had time to scream... she had tried to struggle but the bastard had her in a grip so tight she could hardly breathe, let alone move. Kicking out on the bed he had tied her ankles she was trussed like a spit roast lamb and she was scared.

Pulling Ness roughly to her feet by her bound hands, Mark, still mute and careful to stay behind her, shoved her into an armless chair facing away from the door. He could see the pulse in her neck beating hard, good... he wanted her to be afraid... she needed to know how easy it was to... well... do what he had just done to her.

He walked to the door, locked it and strode back to stand in front of Ness. Pulling up another chair he sat legs stretched out in front of him, arms folded across his tight black T-shirt, her eyes widened. He sat in silence watching her. She hadn't listened to her brother, hadn't heeded his warning or as far as he could tell been in any way changed by his actions. He wanted Ness in no doubt that he was in control, his instructions would be followed... he had promised Kal he would keep her safe and to do that she had to listen... listen and follow instruction... to the letter... she also had to know that it wasn't only her safety at risk.

He leant forward to get his phone from his pocket and dialled still keeping both eyes firmly on her face.

"Got her... putting you on speaker," Mark held up the phone, still watching Ness. His dark inky eyes were narrowed; his face hard and uncompromising. He was broad and menacing, the muscles sharply defined through his T-shirt. Leaning in closer to Ness' face, his eyes never losing contact with hers. Ness swallowed. Uneasy. This guy was no stooge. She lowered her eyes but he tapped her chin, "Look at me!" She looked. "I'm taking this off... don't piss me off by yelling for help," she nodded. Mark pulled down the bandana and tugged the cotton wad from her mouth.

Ness sucked in a huge breath, "Do you know what your sidekick has done to me... he–"

"Not interested!" Kalum cut off Ness' complaint, his voice harsh and controlled. He wasn't frothing at the mouth; it unnerved her.

"Mark will do whatever he thinks necessary... with my full approval... you've picked a formidable foe Ness... for your own sake don't piss him off. He is going to fill you in on some vital details... listen... follow his instruction... TO THE LETTER!"

"But Kalum... he..."

"Shut it Ness! Mark I have to call this in... the chief will be champing at the bit... do what you have to with her..." The line went dead.

Mark raised an eyebrow, "That sounds entertaining," checking his watch he frowned: seven forty. He sat back in the chair, silent again, watching her. He stood and walked to the back of the hut. Ness couldn't see what he was doing. After a couple of minutes he returned holding a mug of steaming coffee. Ness looked at the mug hopefully and when Mark sat down and took a great gulp she gasped.

"You selfish wanker."

He took another gulp before speaking "If you want a coffee... ask nicely," Ness glowered back at him. He waited, but she didn't speak. "I'll take your silence as a negative... okay so the first thing you need to know is Kal and Max's cover story–"

Ness interrupted, "I need a drink."

"Then ask me nicely," Ness kicked out with her bound feet in frustration. Mark tutted and carried on.

"Their names are the same... keeps it uncomplicated... they are married. Max is writing a romance novel and is here for research purposes... the cottage is rented... from a bona fide landlord," he paused to drink some more.

Realising he wasn't going to give in Ness submitted plus she reasoned with herself he would have to untie her.

"Please may I have a coffee... and a smoke?"

"You may," he got up poured her a large mug full placing it on a small wooden table to the side of her, before releasing her arms. "Give them a rub," he rummaged in her bag and pulling out a pack of cigarettes, lit one and placed it on a saucer next to the coffee.

Ness drunk her coffee down in one go before sitting back and taking a large drag on her cigarette. She tapped the ash, wary of Mark watching her closely.

"You could untie me... I'm not going to run."

Mark laughed "You wouldn't get far if you did," He leant in close to her face – the smile gone.

"You should try... give me a reason."

Ness shuddered, to do what she didn't care to know. She shook her head "I won't... I... I... just want to help."

"I don't believe you... I think you want to help yourself... get the story... regardless of who you trample to get it... who's lives you put in danger... who you get killed along the way... as long as Ness gets what she wants... fuck the rest of us... correct?" he sat back watching her. She flushed and lowered her eyes.

"I thought so... guilty as charged... you leave me no choice... I'm sorry, I like and respect your brother – causing him grief gives me no pleasure," he shook his head his face wore a mask of sorrow as he stood up and slowly reached for something hidden at the back of his belt.

Ness panicked, thinking that he was reaching for a gun, sure he was going to shoot her.

"No! I really do want to help... and yes I want the story... but not until it's over... when you're done... when..." Mark stood in front of her legs slightly apart reaching out with his free hand and taking a large handful of hair yanked her head back. Her eyes bulged wide in terror.

"No! Please! I want to help... I'll do whatever you say... I won't write a word without your approval... I'm sorry... I promise... oh god please," Ness wept, genuine tears ran down her face.

Mark gripped her hair tighter and jerking her head back further he stood in silence watching as she cried. Ness squeezed her eyes tight shut; her heart hammered in her chest as she waited for the feel of cold steel against her forehead.

Seconds ticked by; to Ness each one felt like a lifetime. Abruptly Mark roughly let go of her hair. She put her head in her shaking hands and sobbed, deep rasping sobs.

He smiled to himself as he sat down opposite her again. So far so good, she seemed genuine enough and would certainly listen to him now... too scared not too. When he spoke he was firm, in control and in charge.

"Okay... I'm willing to give you one chance... this is it... you do as I say... follow my instructions exactly... you will also follow Kalum's orders... when it's over and if the chief gives his approval... you may have the story... we check over what you have written and nothing gets published without our approval."

Ness raised her head; tears still ran from her red and puffy eyes. Hiccupping, she nodded.

"I want your word Ness... NOW! He slammed his fist on the table. She jumped.

"Yes... Yes I give you my word... I'll do as you both say, follow instructions and won't write anything without approval."

He nodded and reached down, picked up her bag emptying it out onto the table.

"Have a smoke," While Ness was having a cigarette he untied her legs then filled up the sink with icy cold water motioning her over when she had stubbed it out.

"Wash your face sort your eyes out then get changed," he pointed to a pile of clothes sitting on a chair. Ness dunked her face into the icy water until she felt her eyes were almost back to normal then washed her hands. Mark handed her a towel to dry them with.

Ness grabbed the clothes "Where do I get changed?"

"Just there is fine."

"Can you turn your back?"

"No."

Ness, face flaming stripped off to her underwear and quickly scrabbled into the clean dry jeans and T-shirt; he stuffed the muddy clothes into a bag as she removed them and put the bag into the cupboard under the sink.

"Sit down," Ness sat and lit another smoke as Mark made more coffee. He set the mugs on the table and checking his watch spoke sharply to her.

"Keep quiet, drink your coffee and listen carefully... I am going to fill you in briefly... for now... on the story so far... you have to remember exactly what I am about to tell you... your life will depend upon it," Ness sat forward cradling her coffee mug.

Chapter Seven

Dictators ride to and fro upon tigers which they dare not dismount. And the tigers are getting hungry.

– Winston Churchill, While England Slept

Ian sat in his office drinking a weak and near cold coffee, god he missed Max. Reaching into the desk drawer for a cigarette, pausing his hand above the packet of Camel, he frowned, remembering the argument he had had with his wife over his last forbidden smoke and slammed the drawer shut.

Instead he flicked on the intercom and boomed "Fanshaw!"

"Yes, Sir?"

"Any word?"

"No, Sir."

He flicked it off. What the fuck were they doing up there? His instructions had been simple reel her in, call in progress and get the fucking job done. Twenty four hours and no word. Drumming his fingers irritably on the desk top he leafed through the file sitting on top of a stack.

The situation in Europe was dire. не мне had been after the Baltic States for a long time…his plans to unite the USSR had been written up decades ago. Add to that the threat of extreme terrorists ISIS and you had a simmering soup pot of organisations all resolute to destroy the western free world and those that wanted to be a part of that freedom… he studied the photographs heading the file. They were gruesome, perverted, thoroughly sickening and despite reports to the contrary from administrations proclaiming them propaganda, all had been verified as correct.

The chief reached into the desk drawer grabbed his packet of Camel and lit one up… the images were disturbing; men, young and old stripped naked, their mottled skin purple; the genitals had been hacked off and their eyes, in most cases, were wide open, mouths gaping. Frozen in a last agonising scream and hung up by hooks in a neat row, all with bullet wounds to the head. The bullets that eventually killed them must have seemed merciful to the poor bastards waiting to be butchered and distributed. Sold discounted to a starving population… most of whom didn't know where their meat was coming from, they were just grateful to be feeding their family... that they were feeding them with other people's sons and husbands was the sick cruelty of their extremist rulers... and one hell of a way to destroy the evidence of their crimes.

He would bet that the guy who owned the butchers shop was hanging among the meat or had been... if he had objected to the new stock he would have become part of that stock.

If he had a wife and daughters they would now be servicing the Jihadi warriors, any sons who wouldn't fight would have been hanging with their father... the poor bastard was probably made to watch them being tortured and slaughtered before it was his turn.

Turning the page Ian looked upon the happy smiling faces of three ordinary British teenage girls... the photo was taken on a school trip... they were at the ripe age to follow a cause... to be made to feel special... rebellion had taken a vicious turn... in his day those same fifteen year olds would try and get away with a touch of mascara or a bit of lippy hastily applied at the bus stop or school toilet... a sneaky night out to a disco, alibis arranged between them... now it was international flights to strange countries thousands of miles away to live the promised life of a princess... the price of their rebellion as they would have quickly found out was to be married in a hasty ceremony to two, three or possibly more older men... they were sexual slaves to answer whatever types of depravity their Jihadi husbands demanded of them...

baby factories to swell the masses of the warrior ranks... he wondered if they were still smiling or if the stark reality of their situation had hit home... home was a place they would probably never see again... they certainly wouldn't have the freedoms they were used to... a harsh punishment for teenage rebellion... when would parents take control back and actually parent. Would the British girls rule superior over the young girls the Jihadists had taken as spoils of war? He doubted it. Some as young as nine, possibly younger, sold for eight pounds apiece. Communal carnal property for the fighters... the bastards had printed booklets on the handling of sexual slaves, saying it was okay to use pre-pubescent girls for sex. Some of the girls had killed themselves... unable to take the abuse any longer... they had taken the only escape route with whatever they could lay their hands on.

He looked down sadly at the photo depicting the broken blood-stained bodies of two young girls. Twin sisters about eight years old. They were Yazdi and had fled from the terrorists with their family only to be captured before reaching safety. Their father had been beheaded in front of them... he had refused to join the ranks of ISIS... their mother had been gang raped before she was shot in the head... the girls had been taken as spoils of war and used by many before they seen their only escape from hell and jumped holding hands from the top of a bombed out building.

Taking another deep drag he opened the next file.

не мне was a patient and determined man. Biding his time, buying into Europe's banks and big business; banks, gas, retail... nobody had their finger in more pies than him. The chief snorted with contempt. And all with the approval of the government of today... all under the illusion that Russia... no, not Russia... the soviets were eager to join democracy... unite with Europe and become strong allies with the west and the fucking stupid bastards believed it.

The defence force had been cut back to the point it was going to have major difficulties defending the country, not to mention aiding its allies and with a further 2% on the cards for this year, made you wonder whose side the government were on... America had warned Britain against the cutbacks... warned that Britain would be unable to remain equal partners if their forces were not matched equally... Britain would be reduced to a lesser role with no say in major events... its forces instead of leading campaigns, would make up a very small portion of another countries... when that happened there would be no return.

In a nutshell; any more cutbacks to military spending and we may as well put our hands in the air and say here we are take us and our country do what you will with us.

не мне rekeys into British airspace were a cause for concern but again it wasn't anything new. One hundred in the past year. Flew over Cornwall this week... testing Britain's response time... they knew why he was doing it... the same reason he sent in subs to the waters of Scotland... checking response times and peacocking to his stalwart followers pretending his might is bigger than it actually is... other countries had had illegal visits too, Australia had had Russian subs and aircraft in its territories in the last few months although, as usual, the Australian government strongly denied this and then put a blanket ban on the media reporting... seemed to be the calling card of the current Aussie PM... Ban the media reporting on anything you don't want the world and your country to know about and if they do dare report have them investigated on a trumped up charge and threaten a two year jail term... then again, their PMs would appear to change as fast as the wind direction over there... maybe the next one will blow in a change for the better.

He hoped so. Australia had to wake up and see that they were a part of the world and the world was watching them... you can't keep jailing your journalists and their sources for reporting on the illegal activities of a government and its departments... that's not a democracy... it's the start of a dictatorship. Australia, the land of the free... where displaced children...refugees... were killing themselves rather than put up with the physical and sexual abuse they received in that county's offshore processing centres... mostly refugees fleeing warn torn countries that ISIS now held... there was a certain symmetry to the whole sorry affair.

The chief stubbed out his cigarette... too many countries were calling themselves democratic without adhering to the rules of democracy.

The buzzer went off at his elbow.

"What!"

"Kalum on the line for you, Sir."

"About fucking time, where the hell have you been?"

"Sorry, Sir things took a little longer than I anticipated."

"I trust all is in order now."

"Yes, Sir all under control,"

"How did you manage it... much opposition."

"There was but she has the message loud and clear... we, erm, shared the problem... she's with Mark now... there has been a development."

"What?"

"He visited the house, she has definitely been marked as his next victim. He has no idea who she is," Kalum paused. The thought that the next sick video could feature his sister took some swallowing.

"Ness knows his agenda... knows his particular skills and passion... she is resolute. Ness intends to help."

"Will she obey orders, follow direction?"

"Yes, Sir."

"Everybody's cover tight?"

"Yes, Sir… erm, she… erm–"

"Spit it out."

"She wants an exclusive when it's over, approved by you," knowing his chief's feeling for the press, or the hag ridden harpies, as he collectively called the media, Kalum wasn't holding out for approval on this one. If the chief said no, Ness would have to except that no means no.

"She can have it on the conditions that 1: I have ultimate approval on whatever she writes and 2: I decide where it goes."

"Yes, Sir."

"Good… I want regular updates and a speedy progress on this… I need Max back ASAP."

"How's the no smoking?"

"Hurry the fuck up and get Max back to the office."

Ian flicked the off button, leaned back in the deep leather chair and swung it around so he was facing the window. He smiled at the shock he had heard in Kalum's voice as he agreed to the article… his was not a loving relationship with the media… there were the few good friends he trusted within their ranks… but the majority of the hacks he would like silenced forever… those that leaked sensitive information and put the lives of operatives and their families in danger were not servicing the public of any country... since the leaks started the secret services had been in a race against time... a race to pull operations... get operatives to safety... get families to safe locations... they hadn't been able to save all... good men and women had died doing their job protecting their country and their fellow countrymen... parents, brothers, sisters had not returned home after work... it had to stop... the mass leaks... the destabilising of Britain by those crying patriotism whilst practising treachery; those who now march to a different drum.

It was time to turn the tables... turn the tide of rot that would have Britain and it's peoples shackled... but first the people had to wake up and see which direction they were being pushed... reveal who's hand was on their back gently guiding them towards the destabilisation and ultimately the destruction of Great Britain and all it stood for... it wouldn't be the first time powerful and influential members of society had been uncovered as soviet agents... wouldn't be the last time either.

This would work out well... Ness could have the exclusive byline and he would make sure it had everything in it to embarrass не мне... he couldn't deny Flake was his and he would make sure не мне cronies couldn't take Flake out pre or post trial... propaganda was the soviets' best weapon and he had decided to hijack it.

Time as usual wasn't on their side; you could not discount the possibility of two major threats joining together to fight a common cause... it had happened before... WW11 was a prime example... of course one or the other turns when their own goal is achieved...they had to stop it before it came to that... yes time was quintessence... and secrecy was the top of the agenda... he would keep this operation to those involved... no one else must know until it's done, dusted and wrapping their fish and chips. He wasn't big on trust... and the tricky thing at this time was who do you trust? Who had Britain's interests at heart and who was lining their own pockets on empty promises? He would also keep it from his stand in PA... she was too inexperienced to navigate authority. Max, on the other hand, was so much more than a PA. A field agent in her time, she had stopped active service when she found out she was expecting her first child... about a week after Kalum's mum was slaughtered in front of her six year old daughter.

Yes... battle lines were drawn... and as long as the boys truly had Ness on side there shouldn't be a hitch.

You couldn't win every battle but you could, with careful planning, poke the enemy where it hurts most. He reminded himself of his old chief's missive: "with small successes large battles are secured."

For the first time in decades, world freedom was threatened on a gargantuan scale. World events, the rising terror threat, the soviet threat, however fragmented they seemed were intrinsically linked. Britain's bleating sheep who were desperate to get out of the EU must understand that a united Europe stands for so much more than a single currency and an open border, It also stood for safety and an accord... a last barrier to the global threat that was now bullying its people to rip apart their own safety net before, like a bunch of lemmings, they leap into the dark abyss.

There had to be changes to the treaty, he was not disputing that, but essentially they had to remain linked. He looked at his watch. Time he was leaving for this morning's briefing at No. 10... six more months and all of this would be someone else's headache.

Chapter Eight

Think of what our nation stands for,

Books from Boots and country lanes,

Free speech, free passes, class distinction, Democracy and proper drains.

– *Sir John Betjeman*

The sun was high in the sky as Ness walked out from the shady woods. She stood for a moment, one hand against the cool bark of an aged pine and the other shading her eyes as she looked toward the house. It didn't seem possible that she had arrived three days ago... three days that had changed her life forever. Her brother was a spy, her life to date – every sordid nasty detail – was on file, she had been kidnapped, her life threatened and as a result had tenaciously demanded to volunteer as bait to catch a serial killer slash Soviet henchman.

Life was not dull, but then again she mused hers had never been boring... and now... now she had to walk into the house knowing exactly what went on in there and who she was dealing with and act as if she knew nothing... shouldn't be too hard after all she arrived with an ulterior motive... but she knew more now... had a compelling urge to hit back for the young redhead in the video... almost as if she had known her... which she hadn't... but she did know that she had to even the score and bring the sick murdering bastard to justice.

Stepping out from the shadow of trees, Ness walked onto the gravel driveway, aware of at least one pair of eyes watching her progress as she strode toward the front door. Sucking in a deep lungful of clean pine air and throwing her shoulders back, Ness pushed open the Gothic door and made her way through the cool silent house to the study. A movement towards the kitchen quarters caught her eye, she turned her head in time to see Agnes disappearing behind the ancient baize door Ness called out to her.

"Morning, Agnes, beautiful day!"

No reply, but she hadn't expected one. Arriving at the study door Ness knocked, the door swung open and Ewan's pale face smiled at her in welcome.

"Good morning," he paused and hungrily took her in from foot to head lingering on her hair. His hand reached up, the cool fingers brushing Ness' cheek as he took a strand hanging loose from her ponytail and tucked it behind her ear. Forcing herself to ignore the intimate gesture and the shiver of trepidation that ran down her spine, she carried on into the room.

"Good morning Ewan, Sir John. Isn't it a gorgeous day?"

"Your night with friends went well?"

"Just the one friend and her husband, but I'm afraid as usual we were so busy catching up he didn't get much attention, we had far too much wine and enough takeout to feed a small army," Ness smiled at John and sat at her desk.

"Thank you so much for sending Ewan down with clothes for me, it was really kind of both of you and I hope I didn't inconvenience you in any way."

"Not at all. Maybe your friend would like to come for tea one afternoon, she's a writer, I believe?"

"Fancy you knowing that, I'm sure she'd love too. Thank you."

Sir John waved away the gesture with one hand uttering "It's nothing."

Ness" conceited smile didn't wholly cover John's air. Picking up a sheaf of papers sitting next to the computer she glanced at the top sheet, asking as she did so, "Is this today's work?"

"Not unless you speak Russian... that's mine," Ewan held out his hand to Ness for the papers. She handed them over laughing, "No Russian is not my bag... a little high school German is about it for languages," she shrugged her shoulders, adding "I've always felt envious of those who are able to pick up another language easily."

Ewan put the papers in John's desk drawer as he left the room he glanced at John who nodded slightly.

"There you go Miss Gordon... there's today's notes for you... if you don't mind I have some other business to attend to this morning."

She was left alone. Picking up the top sheet Ness gave it a quick glance before she began to type. It was the usual egotistical twaddle encompassing all of Sir Johns professed qualities; intelligence, cunning, daring combined with the physique no woman could resist and enough charisma to challenge '007' at his own game. Ness snorted, quickly turning it into a cough. One thing she was certain of today was that she was being watched. The Russian paper performance was just that, a performance designed to test her. If those papers contained anything of importance she'd be surprised... but she would remember to pass it on to Mark... her fingers slammed the keys... how she could ever have found the bastard attractive... he was a shit.

Well, the quicker I get this crap typed up the sooner I can get out of here and do a little snooping of my own. One of Mark's strict orders was that she was not to snoop, the exact wording had been, "If I catch you trying to search any part of that house without my approval the deal's off and you're out of here," of course she had agreed.

She had also come to her own conclusion that trying to rifle John's study for secrets relating to Moscow was better left to the professionals. If she found anything that could be useful to her brother she would tell him but she had no wish to be shot at in the night, deciding instead to concentrate on finding Ewan's lair. To do that she had to make them believe she was no threat, ensuring she could have free rein to explore without raising any suspicions. Firstly she had to get closer to Flake… make him think she was interested… give his sick mind something to concentrate on and hopefully get him relaxed enough around her for something useful to slip out.

The office door opened and Agnes stuck her head around it to inform Ness lunch was served.

"Goodness… is it that time already? I'll just finish this paragraph and I'll be straight through… thank you Agnes."

Both men were chatty throughout lunch. John asking about Max's book, "What was the plot? Where was it set? Had she had anything else published?" Ness laughed off his questions telling him "It's a historical romance set in the 1800's and that is all I know… romances aren't really my thing… but I do know that she is very interested in looking at your home… so it must fit in with whatever period this was built."

John smiled at Ness saying he would have to invite Max and her husband to tea very soon to satisfy his curiosity. "What is her husband's name... is he a writer too?

"Kalum... No he's not a writer," Ness filled her mouth with food to buy some time, unable to remember what Kalum was supposed to do for a living, she'd just have to improvise and hope for the best, swallowing she continued, "Kalum's more bureaucrat than artisan but a nice guy all the same," and that was a lie because the bastard had not been nice to her at all, she quickly changed the subject.

"I would really like to explore those hills behind the house... they don't look that far... is there anyone who can show me the way? I have an appalling sense of direction; the chances of me finding my way there or back alone is highly debatable," Ness smiled whilst shrugging her shoulders at her own ineptitude.

Ewan's pale face shone with excitement "I would love the pleasure of your company in a walk."

"Thank you Ewan... I'll look forward to it, just let me know when you're free and I'm all yours, maybe we could take a picnic?"

"Splendid idea Ness... I'll arrange everything," his expression was hungry; his tongue slowly ran around his bottom lip as his eyes fell from Ness's and lingered on her breasts, "I'm so looking forward to taking you."

Sir John coughed "Time we went back to work Ewan," the men left telling Ness they would see her for tea.

Ness walked into the grounds and eagerly lit a cigarette making her way around the side of the house. The views really were impressive, in the distance the silhouette of deer could be seen grazing against the backdrop of purple cushioned hills. Under other circumstances she would relish the thought of exploring them. Enticing Ewan on a walk was probably unwise but if she wanted to find out more about him, what made him tick, why he was who he was – it was essential she discovered those things for her exclusive – then it was necessary she spend time with him alone. Make him believe she trusted him had no fear of him, plus, she reasoned with herself, he was unlikely to try anything in the open. He needed his theatre to perform in and she needed to find out where it was and hopefully he would unwittingly supply clues to its whereabouts.

Stubbing out her cigarette, Ness made her way back round to the study. She figured she'd have what was left of today's notes typed up within the hour, then she was going to have a well-deserved nap before tea and after she intended to do a little exploring of the house. After all she had John's permission to do so.

Ness hadn't been in her room since the previous day; it was obvious someone else had and not just to grab her some clothes. The toiletries in the bathroom had been moved, they had sat along the sides of the bath but now they were grouped on one side. Agnes cleaning or snooping, Ness presumed, before heading back into the bedroom and gratefully curling up on the bed, pulling a blanket over her and falling quickly asleep.

The bedroom door silently opened a crack just enough for Agnes to peek in and watch Ness sleep, She wore a harried look and stayed only long enough to ensure the girl was alone and safe.

Agnes wasn't the only one watching Ness, Ewan, from his lair had watched her walk through to the bathroom in the hope she would take a shower, he was disappointed but not for long. Ness stripped down to her underwear before she got into bed. She looked delectable, he was so looking forward to tonight: she was sure to take a bath or shower then. The anticipation at studying her naked flesh intimately, unguardedly was electrifying. He had to be careful though. He had slipped off so he could watch her and wanted no meddling from John. This had to be his secret pleasure, he watched Ness sleeping and he could see the outline of her body under the blanket, the heave of her breasts as she breathed. She yawned and opened her eyes staring straight at him, he blew her a kiss. She stretched and threw back the blanket her long legs swung over the side of the bed. He'd have to go; he couldn't risk John finding out about the camera.

"Ewan," John was waiting at the entrance to the cellar. "I hope you are honouring our agreement... the girl... you do not touch her... or I will make good my promise and inform him that you are no longer safe... a liability to the cause... and you know what that means...."

"John!" Ewan wore a disappointed expression "I assured you I wouldn't harm a hair on her head whilst she is in your employ and I mean to honour our agreement," the very slight flush to Ewan's normally pale cheek didn't go unnoticed. John nodded, "I hope so... for your sake Ewan... I do hope so."

John held a large brown envelope in one hand he gestured with it to Ewan.

"The list is here... we should get started."

"Of course... the mail's late today," Ewan walked through the door and carried on up the stairs, John following closely behind, shut the door after him.

"Worth waiting for to maintain secrecy... hand typed documents posted through the regular mail is the only way to assure our work remains covert... you know that."

"Yes... yes of course... I only meant if our documents were posted direct it would save time...."

John cut him off. "You know as well as I do that the system exists to maximise security and avoid suspicion. If we constantly received large envelopes

114

from Moscow it would raise questions... the envelopes are sent to a middle man of no consequence in the UK who then posts them onto us."

"And if he opens it before sending it on?"

"Then we would know... all he has to do is remove the topmost envelope, add postage and forward... if he opens the contents he breaks the seal... we find out and inform Moscow," Johns lip curled into a cruel sneer "And as I have said he is of no consequence... he meets with an accident... maybe when he is waiting for a train he slips... or falls from a height... possibly he has been suicidal for a while and no-one knew until it was too late... so sad for the families... but that's life."

"Then we have to find a new post-man."

"We run four at a time... they don't know of each other... we rotate... each man gets a job once a month... they are well paid... this post-man would have collected his pay once he had posted the envelope..."

Ewan tittered, "A money transfer...that poses risks."

John stopped where he stood. "Are you being purposefully stupid today? The money is left at an agreed hiding place... it could be in a rubbish bag in a bin... or in a false rock sitting under a bush... the post men do not meet each other... their handler takes care of the payment... they have no contact with him after the initial meetings."

"And if they want a pay rise or feel they have been discovered?"

"As I have said... they are of no consequence and accidents happen every day. Now can we please get on with the job in hand," waving the envelope under Ewan's nose, John led the way to the library.

Ewan followed, smiling. Of course he already knew most of what John had told him but it had served a purpose, John was no longer interested in what Ewan was doing in the cellar for so long.

Ness had woken refreshed from her nap. Splashing her face with cold water and getting dressed she decided against making a coffee in her room instead venturing out to meet Agnes in her own territory, which Ness presumed was the kitchen. If she wasn't there it was a good opportunity to meet other members of the household staff, glean a little information over a friendly cuppa.

But first a cigarette – she'd just nip out the front door. Ness had turned the corner, about to head down the staircase when voices drifted up to her. They were slightly muffled, but as they came closer Ness recognised Ewan and John.

Stepping back, concealing herself in a shadowy alcove by the stairs she held her breath and listened.

Interesting conversation and one that would need to be conveyed to her brother or Mark... it couldn't hurt to know how information and instructions were passed; they may know already but she would tell them what she had found out. The library was definitely on her list of places to explore and as John was a known bibliophile she had a good excuse, one she hoped was above suspicion. Ness waited until their footsteps had retreated down the passage before letting go of her breath and continuing down the stairs. She smiled to herself as she sucked in the smoke of her cigarette sitting in the sunshine on the front steps. Good old fashioned eavesdropping with a human ear was definitely a match for Moscow's method of bypassing electronic surveillance.

Buoyed by an unexpected success Ness was in good spirits as she made her way through the baize covered door and down a gloomy windowless corridor heading to where she presumed the kitchen was.

Ness had opened three doors leading to storage rooms and what must have been the butler's pantry from the house's hay-day before she came across the kitchen. Should she knock or walk in... deciding on the latter, Ness opened the door and snatches of conversation floated out. A woman's voice she hadn't heard before plus one she couldn't ever confuse after the past 24 hrs. Mark... too late to turn back, Ness opened the door wide and standing on the threshold cleared her throat.

"Um... is it okay to come in?"

A grey-haired plump Scottish woman wrapped in an apron that strained across her massive bosom was laying tea things onto a long scrubbed wooden table, she stopped and smiled at Ness.

"Come away in pet... I was jist getting yer tea ready..." she ruffled Mark's hair, "and gieing this scallywag a wee bite ta keep him going."

Chapter Nine

Defence, not defiance.

Motto of the Volunteers Movement, 1859

Ness crossed the threshold and stood on the stone flagged floor, pleased at the friendly welcome. "Would it be okay if I had my tea in here with you? I'm not sure where John and Ewan are and the dining room is a bit…" she left off and made her way further into the kitchen.

"Of course ye can pet, sit yerself doon and get something doon ye afore it's all gone," she smacked Mark's hand away as he reached for another slice of chocolate cake.

"Where are your manors laddie… offer the lassie first," tutting, she placed a cup and saucer in front of Ness along with a plate and knife then busied herself setting a tray for two.

"Jist as well ye found us... the men are having a confab in the library... some new book Sir John had delivered this afternoon," snorting she carried on piling the tray with cake, scones and sandwiches.

"Why he has to spend so much time and money on dusty dirty old books I'll never know," a fresh plate of sandwiches was placed by Ness's elbow followed by a plate of delicious looking scones with jam and cream. Ness eagerly added both to her tea plate and filling her cup from the large pot on the table got stuck in, she was famished, she just hadn't realised it until she had sat down.

Agnes came into the kitchen from what must be the back door and stopped in her tracks on seeing Ness seated at the table.

"Miss Gordon... I wondered where you had got too... you weren't in your room when I knocked."

"Sorry Agnes... I got lonely so I went in search of company... was there anything in particular you wanted?"

"You received a phone call when you were napping... your friend Max says you left your mobile phone at their place... she says she's not particularly busy this evening if you'd like to nip down and collect it later on after dinner."

"Thank you Agnes... I was hoping for an early night... maybe it can wait until tomorrow," Ness glanced sideways at Mark, Agnes mistaking the look added "Maybe Mark can collect it for you... save you the walk," Agnes looked at Mark expectantly.

"Sorry Miss... I have a previous engagement this evening," He smiled first at Agnes then at Ness. Ness didn't miss the icy glint in his eye. He carried on. "But if the young lady is tired I have a bicycle she can use... if you'd care to come with me, Miss, after tea, I can sort it out for you."

"Thank you Mark... I'm sure Miss Gordon is appreciative of the offer," Agnes looked expectantly at Ness who agreed.

Agnes left with the tea tray for the library and the cook planted herself down at the table, helping herself to tea and scones. Ness carried on eating avoiding Mark's eye.

The whole situation was absurd. Here she was eating chocolate cake with a man who had wanted to put a bullet through her head only this morning, if it had been yesterday she would have joyfully jumped at the chance of spending time alone with him in a dark garage but today she knew what he was and what he was capable of. A skilled agent and proficient killer whose eagle eye was firmly set on her and her actions.

Ness shivered. She'd never been a coward... she had been in many a tight spot before, some would say dangerous... but the thought of being alone with this man wasn't sending pleasurable thrills through her... but... she had to realistic... she had information to pass on... a job to do... a story to work on and a ridiculous need that she couldn't understand to prove herself to him... so... she would bloody well have to pull herself together and get on with the job in hand.

Mark was watching Ness unobtrusively whilst listening to the cook who was reminiscing about the house's grand past when she was a girl.

He wondered if he gone too far this morning... she was a little pale and was mechanically eating looking at the cook, but if she'd heard a word the woman was saying he'd be surprised... then again... her life had been turned inside out and upside down in the past 24 hours... it can't have been easy for her... but it had been necessary... crucial even... no, he had not gone too far... it was the first time such a thought had even entered his head... thoughts like that were not allowed in his head... he had a job to do... treating Ness with kid gloves was not going to keep her safe... she was a danger to herself... she had no fail-safe... no sense of danger... he was her reminder that danger was close at hand... and her protection...

The cook had finished her story and rising to her feet, started to collect the empty tea things.

"Well I'll be getting on young Mark here will take ye and sort ye oot a bicycle Ness."

Mark stood and gave the cook a peck on the cheek, "Delicious as usual, if you were only single I'd marry you."

"Ach away wie ye, that's yer stomach blethering," she laughed.

"Come along then, Miss, I'll sort you out a bike," Mark nodded towards the back door and Ness followed. The door opened onto stone steps that led up from the basement kitchen to an open area where the bins sat, a winding stone pathway followed a line of bushes and opened out onto what must have been the stable block. Three large stables stood in an L shape set around a cobbled square. A handsome horse whinnied through the half open stable door and was answered by its neighbour in the next stall. Mark gestured towards the end of the L shape and the stable that now housed odds and ends including a ride on lawn mower, and the promised bicycle.

It was dark inside the stable and it took Ness a moment to adjust after the bright sunshine outside. She stood inside the door way as Mark headed towards the back of the room moving aside boxes until he reached his target.

"Come and see what you think, Miss... it should do you."

It was the first time he had spoken since they had left the kitchen. Walking over to him and squatting by his side she whispered, "I have something to tell you..." He cut her off with a warning gesture raising a finger to his lips and slightly shaking his head. She understood and silently nodded adding "It looks fine... can we take it outside and have a proper look?"

Back in the courtyard Ness held the bike whilst Mark gave it an oil and checked the brakes.

"They don't make them like this anymore... last forever one of these will," he continued to adjust the brakes.

"That should do it, just hop on, Miss, and we can adjust the seat height."

Ness sat on the seat; her feet could just reach the ground if she stood on tiptoe.

"I think this will be fine... I'll just take her for a test run down the drive and then back here."

"Sure thing, Miss," Ness peddled across the courtyard, turned the corner and carried on down the long driveway. It was actually enjoyable, she admitted to herself and by the time she had got back to the courtyard her cheeks were flushed and the wind had ruffled up her hair. She jumped off laughing.

"It's great! Thanks Mark."

He stood close to her, one hand on the handle bars and leaning in to check the lights worked, his dark head bent over he spoke in a low voice.

"Don't stand us up tonight Ness... I'll be following closely behind you."

She hissed back crossly "Why would I do that? I have information to pass on," not giving him a chance to answer she went on louder "That's perfect, thank you so much," and wheeling the bike away from him, she jumped back on and peddled quickly off.

Mark looked on lustily at Ness's retreating rear, thoughts like that just wouldn't do... no Sir... not at all. Whipping out a rag from his back pocket he wiped his oily hands and said aloud, "Ah well back to work." Parking her bike at the front of the house Ness was about to go inside when Ewan and John came out.

"Ah, Miss Gordon...we have to go into town I'm afraid you'll have to dine alone this evening," Sir John sounded most apologetic.

"That's okay," Ness smiled at them both, "I hope you don't mind me using your bike."

"Not at all... feel free," John climbed into the driver's side of the four wheel drive. Ewan grabbed Ness's hand in his and raising it to his lips looking into her eyes slowly and deliberately kissed it before seating himself beside John.

"I'll see you tomorrow Ness... be careful on that contraption... I would hate you to fall off and hurt yourself... don't forget our picnic date... I thought tomorrow afternoon if the weather remains fine."

"Lovely Ewan... I'll look forward to it," Ness waved them off smiling. As soon as they had gone through the gates and out of sight she wiped her hand on her jeans.

Ugh… what a creep… Walking back into the house Ness wondered where to start her search. Better make sure Agnes is not around first; it wouldn't do to be discovered snooping by her. As if in answer Agnes appeared from the kitchen quarters. Ness watched her as she made her way upstairs. If Agnes was upstairs it made sense to start downstairs – her eye fell upon the door John and Ewan had emerged from earlier. Good a place to start as any she supposed, quietly opening the door and pulling it to behind her. She felt along the wall with the back of her hand until she came to a light switch. Flicking the switch a bare bulb illuminated a dim passageway at the foot of worn stone steps. Carefully and quietly she headed down them.

The stairs opened up onto a wide cellar floor. Bare bulbs hung from the ceiling, casting a dim orange glow onto wooden racks filled with dusty bottles. Ness moved amongst them across the stone floor sending dust into the air that spiralled in the patches of light.

Where to begin? Ness moved methodically amongst the racking, checking the cellar and stopping periodically to read a label on a bottle. John had expensive tastes. There were vintage wines, brandies and bottles of whiskey, some covered in a fine layer of dust. The further back she ventured the dustier the racking. Boxes sat against the walls along with a couple of old trunks. More booze, she thought as she wandered slowly to the back of the cellar. Nothing –

just an old rickety book case sitting against the back wall. Turning, Ness looked around her; something had to be in here: why else would both of them be down here?

Ness moved towards the trunks and opening the lid again, lifted out dusty sacking... maybe they had hidden something in the trunks. Putting aside any qualms she felt about sticking her hand deep into the dark interior she fished about; her hand came upon something soft lifting it out she looked at it with a sinking feeling. A colourful shoulder bag a little dirty with age. With a shaking hand she sat on the neighbouring trunk and slowly opened the bag. Lifting out a purse she laid it by the side of her. Then there was a small address book-cum-diary, a hairbrush and a makeup bag containing some cheap and slightly garish lipstick, a mascara, a packet of panty liners, lip gloss and a compact mirror. Feeling slightly sick, Ness carefully laid out the contents. The hairbrush still had hairs stuck in the bristles, long bright red hairs. Swallowing back the tears Ness carefully plucked a few hairs from the brush, careful to leave some in place she wrapped them in a clean tissue from her pocket and tucked them safely away. Ness pocketed the diary... that could be useful. Putting the rest of the girl's treasures back in the bag she was careful to put everything back into the trunk in the order she had got it out.

The fucking murderous bastard... anger replaced sorrow and with new determination she made another

127

sweep of the cellar exploring every corner. Nothing else... but there had to be... her eye fell on the bookcase. Why would there be an empty bookcase in a wine cellar? Moving across to it she stood in front and checked it from all angles. Was it the dim light or did one side stick out more than the other? Gently Ness pulled the bookcase; it moved easily away from the wall revealing its secret, a small, cobwebby passageway.

Gingerly, Ness entered the passageway, feeling her way along the wall. It came to an abrupt end. In front of her was old sack cloth stuck to the wall. She pushed it aside, astounded to find herself faced with a bright shiny metal door and a modern key coded lock.

Heart pounding, Ness made her way back along the passage... she wasn't stupid trying to gain entry, it would be pointless and she didn't know if the door was alarmed... she just wanted to get the hell out of the cellar as quickly as possible.

Making sure everything was as she found it before heading up the stairs. Ness flicked off the light switch and, opening the door a crack, listened... nothing... as slowly as her racing heart would allow she got through the door, closing it behind her... stopping and listening again before she made her way up the stairs and into the relative safety of her room.

It was essential that she remain calm and act as usual... she couldn't afford to raise any suspicion... her life depended on it. Walking into the bathroom and splashing her face and hands with cold water she hummed a tune... they would definitely have some sort of listening device, she knew that... best keep her finds hidden where they were until she could safely unload them onto her brother this evening... dare she skip dinner here and head to the village or would it be risky... no, better stick to the plan... she would head down this evening straight after dinner and in the mean time she needed a strong coffee half a dozen cigarettes and she would sit on the balcony with them... at least she could appear calm on the outside.

Steaming hot coffee in one hand and a smoke in the other, Ness sat in the early evening sunshine giving an excellent impression of an unruffled and tranquil woman without a care in the world. Inside she was seething with hatred and a contempt unknown to her before; hatred for a man so vile he could take out an innocent life with such obvious enjoyment.

Contempt for those who ruled, who sought his services for their own political drives and prosperity.

Ness glanced at her watch. Time to head down for dinner... at least the ghouls were out tonight... huh... Flake... he was heading for a meltdown... she would make sure of that.

Words came into her head from a counselling session when she was a teenager, "Channel and use your anger for productive purposes," she had never understood those words until today... she would not recoil in fear or run away... instead she would remember the little redhead... and use that anger against her executioner…she would not be his next victim… no-one would.

Ness sat at the large dinner table alone, forcing herself to smile and exchange polite chatter with Agnes as she served each course; chewing slowly, methodically, trying not to think of what she had hidden in her pocket. If she thought about it swallowing the food would be impossible. Chewing was hard enough. At last it was over. Declining coffee, saying she would have one at Max's, she was able to leave. Stopping to light a cigarette before putting the packet in the bike's wicker front basket she peddled off down the long drive, heading toward the village. It wasn't until she was well away from the house that she realised, she had no bloody idea how to get to the house from the road.

Should she stop and ask directions… but unless sheep could talk that idea was a no-brainer… the road was empty… if she followed the direction of the wood it should take her close to the house. Keeping an eye to the field of sheep on her left she followed the line of the wood directly behind it. Mark said he would be following behind her. She checked: no-one… bloody typical…you want him he's not around… you don't want him he's pouncing on you from behind… where the fuck was he… hang on…was that someone ahead… yes it was him.

Mark was sauntering slowly along the quiet road she quickly caught up with him and rang her bell. He stepped onto the grass embankment as if to let her pass. She slowed down as she came level with him he raised a hand in greeting and smiling a hello told her to take the next turning on the left and follow the road. To anyone watching it looked like a polite good evening. She signalled a left turn and carried on.

The road was more like a large lane; trees lined either side and cast shadows of dappled sunlight across her path. Birds were singing in the trees and smells of summer drifted past her as a tractor chuntered sluggishly across the field on her right.

It was all so surreal... the beauty around here, the ordinary every day country goings on, and just up the lane in a Gothic eyesore lurked an evil so cruel, so abhorrent, it had to be crushed... she was going to help bring the bastard down. Parking her bike in front of the house Ness dismounted and with a sinking heart realised she still had a massive six plus foot stumbling block to cross... her brother... he wouldn't have forgiven this morning's great escape and she was too exhausted physically and mentally to argue with him... hopefully what she had in her pocket would convince him she was trustworthy... she had brought it to him hadn't she... didn't that deserve forgiveness?

Chapter Ten

What does national unity mean? It surly means that reasonable sacrifices of party opinions, personal opinion and party interest, should be made by all in order to contribute to the national security.

– *Winston Churchill, 1939*

The door opened before Ness could knock. Max stood smiling on the threshold.

"Come in Ness… I've just made a pot of coffee."

"That sounds lovely… what do you think of my new wheels?

Ness walked into the hall and through to the kitchen Max closed the door and followed. She had just set one foot into the kitchen when her brother swooped down on her. Stepping back in alarm at the rage on his face she stood on Max's foot. Max squealed and Kalum grabbed Ness' shirt front and propelled her into a kitchen chair. Standing legs spread in front of her one sinewy arm on either side of the chair he bent his head until they were nose to nose. His breathing was hard, ragged, his dark eyes were virtually black they pierced into Ness'. She swallowed hard and when it became apparent he was not going to speak, she tentatively cleared her throat and spoke softly.

"Er Kalum... I know you're mad at me... I'm sorry for running off this morning... it was a stupid thing to do... I'm not proud of my past behaviour... I do really mean it...I intend to help and not just because your sidekick threatened to kill me... I have changed... I'll do as you say...well maybe not all the time but definitely most of the time," Still no response just that uncompromising hard stare Ness swallowed nervously. Was he going to make her go home, locking her up until he could take her back himself? If that was his idea it was not going to happen. Ness looked him straight in the eye with a confidence she didn't feel and calmly dropped her bombshell, there was no way he'd send her home after this.

"I found Flake's torture chamber and evidence that the girl was there... I also know how information and instructions gets passed between them and Moscow... Ness held her breath and studied his face for a reaction... nothing... Er, Max I think a stray ray of sunlight must have hit my brother... he appears to have turned to stone... Kalum, it's been a long day... I'm tired I have a lot to tell you... I would love a coffee and…" Ness took a risk and pushed at his chest. "Some personal space."

The back door opened and Mark walked in. "Aw…another family bonding session… you want to use my belt this time Kal?"

"What! No… No…" Ness cried out in alarm Kalum's lip twitched he stood upright folded his arms across his chest and spoke. "Let's hear what you have to say first."

"What do you mean first…you are so unfair… give me a break for fuck's sake," He stood watching her face for a moment then moved back motioning her to the table. Ness stood and gently fished the wad of tissue from her pocket followed by the small notebook also wrapped in tissue. Placing both on the table she sat down again, gratefully wrapping her cold fingers around the mug of hot sweet coffee Max had placed on the table.

Drinking deeply from the mug Ness took a few moments to relax herself before beginning.

"I was standing hidden from view at the top of the stairs when I overheard John and Ewan talking…" Ness began by telling them how communications from Moscow were received, the simplicity of the arrangement would make it difficult to track down whichever middleman they were currently using, Mark interrupted.

"That's valuable Ness… very useful… We can get the chief onto that one," he looked to Kalum for agreement Kalum nodded and told Ness to carry on.

"I wanted to look around so I started in the cellar…" she paused and drew in a breath before explaining the layout of the cellar with its rows of dusty bottles and old trunks and boxes sitting along the walls. How she noticed the bookcase was out of place in its surroundings and how she had found the hidden passage with the concealed door at the end with its combination lock. She then went on to explain how she had explored the contents of the trunks and what she had found.

Very gently Ness unwrapped the package containing the long red hairs laying it out on the table top she unwrapped the diary and carefully placed it next to the hair.

Draining what was left of her coffee Ness lit a cigarette.

"I was very careful… I wasn't seen going into or leaving the cellar… I didn't disturb anything and put the contents of the trunk back in the same order I took them out… I took a few hairs off the brush and put it back… I think this is proof that she was there… I can draw you a map of the cellar and…" she paused. How would Kalum and Mark react when she told them of the planned picnic date in the hills… "Flake has agreed to show me around the hills. We're taking a picnic… I may pick up more information… and he's unlikely to do anything to me just yet… I mean everyone knows I'm going with him... When I know when we're going, he..." she thumbed at Mark, "can always follow us... she sighed heavily... look, I just thought it might prove useful... and John's invited you and Max to come for tea one day and to look around the house for research for your book, Max..." Ness lit another cigarette, waiting for all sorts of hell to be unleashed on to her... three stunned faces stared at her in total silence. Kalum was the first to speak.

"You positive you weren't seen... by anyone?"

"Positive! John and Ewan left this afternoon after tea... I thought it may have something to do with the communication they received today... Agnes was in her room, napping probably, with the help of a large scotch...."

Max refilled Ness' mug. "I think you have done remarkably well... maybe you can arrange for us to come for tea tomorrow..." Max looked to Kalum for agreement he nodded.

"Good idea Max... an invite to look around the house with Ness' new information means we can get on top of this quickly... I thought I had given you a no snooping rule, Ness."

"I wasn't snooping, I was given free rein to explore... so I explored... If I wanted to snoop I would have gone straight to the study and looked through the sheaf of papers written in Russian that were so obviously placed to tempt me if I had been working for an intelligence agency... and since we

136

know the study has hidden cameras it would have been remarkably stupid of me," Ness snapped back at Kalum "Anyway if there is anything to find the library would be the place, as that's where they dispense instructions from Moscow."

Ness looked at her watch "Look Kalum... I'm tired. All I want to do is get into a hot bath before I fall into bed... can we get on and save the recriminations for when I have more time and energy to fight my case?"

Kalum nodded, "It can wait," Ness glared at him as he fished her phone out of his pocket and placed it on the table.

"Your phone – with a few modifications. Listen carefully... I have built in a tracker... we will know where you are at all times of the day and night."

Ness interrupted, "Good."

Kalum, ignoring the interruption, carried on, "If you are in trouble there is an emergency button..." Kalum pointed to a small purple jewel embedded on the back of the phone case. "looks like a piece of phone bling... depress it and your phone connects straight to our phones and the chief's... we can listen to you, hear what's happening and get to you within minutes... if you are at all concerned for your safety press it... all of your incoming and outgoing calls will be monitored... I think that's about it..."

"What, no self-destruct? No laser gun or hidden cavity with a handy cyanide pill? Ooh what about..."

"Need I remind you it is my decision if you walk out of that door or I carry you kicking and screaming up the stairs and believe me," Kalum leant into Ness his face inches from hers. "this time you won't get away... so are you going to behave... or..."

Ness held up both hands in mock surrender. "Okay... for goodness' sake... lighten up."

Mark was on his feet before Kalum could react. "I think it's time I escorted Ness back to the house... I'm sure she understands what's at stake," he looked pointedly at Ness. She got the meaning. Her big brother may play the heavy handed patriarch but taunting Mark was a far more dangerous game to play.

"In a minute, Mark," Kalum sat back in his chair and studied Ness. Puzzled, he ran his hand through his hair ruffling it up. The look Mark had sent Ness was a warning, a warning that she had heeded straight away... Mark had achieved in twenty hours what he had failed to do In twenty years... he watched as Ness lit a cigarette and sent a look of withering contempt at Mark's turned back... it looked like his unruly sister had met her match... and she was furious about it... he grinned.

"What are you smiling at... you look demented."

"Just pleased things have gone well, Ness... so far so good... I'm not convinced going with Flake to such an isolated place is a good idea..." He raised his hand as she opened her mouth to protest "I don't think it's a good idea but that doesn't mean I'm going to stop you... you've done well today... I don't want you getting cocky... you keep your phone on you within easy reach at all times... as soon as you know the date, time and route you tell one of us... don't be too inquisitive and don't go looking for trouble, Ness... it'll find you soon enough." He turned in his chair to Mark.

"You ready?"

Mark was standing by the sink gargling with a blended whiskey. "Nearly... just adding a finishing touch," He sprinkled a little of the whiskey down the front of his T-shirt and turned.

"All done... Right Ness... you leave from the front and I'll catch up with you on the road... this for me Max?" picking up a carrier bag from the kitchen side he opened it and sniffed.

"My favourite after a night down the pub... egg fried rice and beef in black bean sauce with a spring roll on the side... you know me too well Max... and it's always appreciated." He planted a kiss on her cheek. Max seeing Ness confused look laughed and explained that the gargling with scotch and the take-out was validation to Mark's cover story that he had been down the pub and caught up with her on the road.

Kalum and Max stood arms around each other as they watched Ness peddle down the moonlit lane. Kalum gently kissed Max before they turned and went inside. The lengths they went to maintain their cover was astounding, thought Ness. Anyone watching would see a couple in love waving off a friend... she would get to the road and meet up with a pissed gardener swinging a bag of take-out... if they were being watched there would be nothing seen to ring alarm bells.

"Miss! Miss Gordon!" Ness turned. Mark half walked, half staggered toward her as she waited, one leg either side of her bike. "I thought it was you Miss... I'll walk you back... pretty young lady like you shouldn't be wandering dark roads alone at night," He delved into the take-out bag and triumphantly pulled the spring roll out staggering as he tried to stay upright, holding onto the bike with one hand as he bit into the roll. Offering it to Ness he staggered further forward grabbing at her for support growling in her ear as he lurched.

"Car 100 metres on the left partially hidden by trees... they're watching... stick close to me... look like I'm pissing you off... shouldn't be hard for you."

"Do ya like working for Sir John, Miss... he's a good boss... pays well... I love my job, Miss... do you, Miss... great food... outdoor life for me... you've got a lovely arse, Miss... looks good on a bike," Mark kept up the babble past the car and on up the driveway of the house. By the time Ness reached the front door she was fuming; if they were still being watched, the watchers would have no doubt that Mark was pissing her off.

Wearily Ness climbed the stairs and let herself into her room. Heading straight for the bathroom she ran a bath adding plenty of bubble bath. As the bath filled up Ness wondered into the bedroom and started to strip. Discarding each item untidily on the floor she crossed naked back into the bathroom and bent over the bath to test the temperature of the water. Turning to the mirror Ness piled her hair high on her head securing it with a clip before gratefully sinking into the hot tub. Picking her sponge from the side of the bath and lathering it well with soap, Ness began to wash the grime of the day from her body before laying back in the suds and closing her eyes with a sigh of pleasure, enjoyed the feel of the hot water on her body.

Deep in the bowels of the house another was enjoying the pleasure of Ness' bath.

Ewan sat glued to the screen; watching with delight as Ness slowly stripped in front of the camera, totally unaware of her audience and the pleasure she afforded it. Her jeans and top lay on the floor. Reaching behind her back with both hands Ness deftly unclipped her bra; both full firm breasts came suddenly into view as the bra cascaded to the floor. Her nipples were erect and rosy pink. Ewan leaned into the screen slowly licking one nipple then the other. Hooking her thumbs into the side of her underpants Ness pulled them down over her thighs exposing her pubic mound. He ran his finger over it, imagining her soft supple flesh opening to his touch, he sucked her imaginary wetness from his finger watching as her pants joined her bra on the floor.

Ness turned and began walking to the bathroom, Ewan smiled he was right... her bottom was a perfect heart shape. He cupped each cheek through the screen. Ness bent over the bath and Ewan ran his finger over her exposed vagina. He imagined his fingers, his hand reaching into its dark depths, pushing in and out as hard and as deep as he wanted... Ness began to climb into the bath one leg over the side Ewan cupped her vagina in one hand and slid the tip of his thumb over her anus... that was something else he liked to play hard with... she was laying in the bath... licking dry lips Ewan watched as she slowly soaped her body... watched as the suds slid down her breasts and a long tendril of hair came loose from its clip falling gently over one nipple. He watched as the bubbles began to vanish and Ness finally climbed out. The bubbles clinging to her slowly slid down her naked flesh, grabbing a fluffy towel Ness patted herself dry then walked naked back into the bedroom. Her skin was pink and glowing from the hot bath. She wrapped a robe around herself and headed out onto the balcony, lighting a cigarette she sat in the cool evening breeze... It was obvious to him that she had enjoyed his attentions as much as he had.

Stubbing out her cigarette, Ness stepped back into the room. Discarding the robe, she tumbled naked into bed, too exhausted to grab clean nightclothes and within seconds she was asleep.

Flake continued to watch Ness sleep. Under the thin sheet her nipples stood out like little peaks. He could see the dark triangle of hair between her legs. She rolled over, hooking the sheet under her knee and taking it with her as she rolled. With one leg bent up in front of her and the other laying straight Flake clapped his hands in joy as he contemplated her bottom raised just enough to bare her labia and anus for his pleasure... dare he risk it... to creep up there and touch her... yes he'd do it.

Meeting no-one on his way, keeping to the shadows of the old house, Flake crept forward slowly taking one stair at a time, reaching Ness' room and taking out a key from his pocket he inserted it in the lock and very slowly turned it. Gently pushing the door open he stood on the threshold the moon illuminated Ness in the same position... he could smell her scent... moving like a cat on the hunt, he was by her side in seconds... bending low so he was level with her head he leant in and gently lifted a strand of hair... pulling a pair of small sharp scissors from his jacket pocket he placed her hair within the shining blades and cut... holding the long tress to his face he inhaled deeply before placing it carefully in his pocket... what to do now? She hadn't woken... a closer look at her exposed flesh... he had to know what he was going to work with... moving quietly he knelt level with her bottom and cautiously moved the sheet until she was completely uncovered from the waist down...he wanted to touch... dare he risk it... he still had the scissors in his hand. Would she wake if the cold steel touched her warm flesh? He leant in and slowly ran the edge of the scissors across her labia. She shivered. He smiled and ran the scissors across her warm flesh again, stopping at the entrance to her vagina, he dipped the sharp tip and held it there... the temptation to thrust the blade into her soft flesh was getting hard to resist... if she rolled over now the choice would be made for him... but that would spoil his plans... he was so looking forward to their special time together... he held his head on one side as he contemplated the shining metal illuminated in the moonlight against her warm flesh before slowly retracting the scissors and putting them in his pocket with the hair... she murmured something and rolled over... he could have sworn she had called his name... few knew him by Flake... maybe he was mistaken... maybe not... she was lying on her back, one leg bent up and out. The sheet had covered her again; he picked up a corner and lifted it off her... he wanted her naked... spread out before him... he would claim her cunt... sucking in a mouthful of saliva he bent low until his lips were almost touching her clitoris and he spat... cocking his head to one side he watched as his saliva hit its mark and trickled down her labia...

Back in the hidden room of the cellar Flake replayed the footage over and over again. He couldn't wait for John's memoirs to be finished... the sooner the better... as soon as they were done, Ness was his to do with as he pleased... he would play this footage to her as soon as he had her strapped in... oh yes... he couldn't wait to get his tongue inside her... properly this time... wrap it round her clit and suck until her clit is sucked right out of her pussy then he would hold it to her lips and make her eat it... he thought he could make her last a day and a half at the very least... I think I'll suggest going on that walk tomorrow afternoon... he relished the thought of spending time alone with her... watching her every move, knowing what her naked flesh looked and tasted like... and she had no idea... he would take her to where they buried the other one... see what she thought of her final resting place... and this was only the beginning... so many things to look forward to... he sat back in the chair and with his head on one side and pressed play again.

Chapter Eleven

O What a tangled web we weave,

When first we practise to deceive!

– *Sir Walter Scott*

Ness woke to the high pitched buzzing of a phone alarm. Rolling over, her hand reached out and fumbled across the bedside table until she felt her hard phone case under her fingers. Pulling it to her she checked the time. 6am! What the fuck was her brother playing at? It's not as if she had to get to the office... but now she was wide awake; her tongue was glued to the roof of her mouth... coffee, that's what she needed. Memories of the most bizarre dream floated hazily around her head... a man was making love to her... she couldn't see him, just feel him... it had been sensually stimulating... erotic dreams where you felt the pleasure in sleep... she had heard of them but never experienced one before... maybe it was some sort of unconscious stress relief... what man would she have dreamed up... please god not Mark... that would be too humiliating... even if he didn't know about it, she would.

Climbing out of bed, Ness pulled on her robe, flicked the switch on the kettle and made a large pot of coffee. Taking it out onto the balcony she sat enjoying the cool early morning breeze. What was she going to do until 10am? She was restless and wanted to get straight back on the case... maybe she could start work early. There wasn't much left to do on John's memoirs, maybe she should slow down... stretch it out... give the guys time to find what they needed. A shout from below had her leaning over the balcony wall.

"Morning, Miss! It's going to be a beautiful day," Mark saluted as he walked past, pushing a large wheelbarrow.

Ness watched his retreating back. Why did he have to be so toned and muscled? Bloody good looking really... but she wasn't thinking of him in that way anymore... he threatened her with a gun for fuck's sake... locked her up... manhandled her... God please don't let him be the man in my dream! Mark had stopped to pick up a spade. He turned and smiled up at her. She blushed scarlet, stubbed out her cigarette and fled in side... his laughter followed through the open window.

Half an hour later Ness was showered, dressed and sitting alone at the breakfast table eating her way through bacon and eggs when the door opened and Ewan strutted through.

"Morning Ness, did you sleep well?" He sat opposite her, pouring himself a glass of orange juice. He looked absurdly happy.

"Yes thank you Ewan. Isn't it a beautiful day? What have you got planned for today?" Why the hell did she ask him that? He immediately looked suspicious, his sharp eyes held menace as he asked in silky tones

"Why do you need to know my plans, Miss Gordon?"

Fuck! "Well it's such a lovely day, I was hoping if you weren't too busy and Sir John was agreeable to my starting work early... we could maybe go exploring and take a picnic lunch," smiling into his face, holding his eyes with hers she hoped he couldn't detect her fear of discovery. What he saw seemed to satisfy him.

"Oh... Oh of course, what a splendid idea," he clapped his hands together in joy," I'll speak to John myself and maybe you can organise the lunch. Yes splendid idea, Ness... marvellous." The door opened and John walked in. Helping himself to a full breakfast, he sat.

"Good morning Miss Gordon... a fine day."

"John!" Sir John looked up at Ewan

"Yes Ewan," He was flushed this morning; had the look of the hunter about him... he had better be sticking to his promise... any sign he wasn't playing ball and Moscow would be informed... there would be someone else waiting in the ranks to take Ewan's place... the party had to be protected at all costs.

"Since it is such a beautiful day and you were only saying yesterday that Ness would be finished with your memoirs in a few days... then she'll be gone from us forever," Pausing for breath Ewan looked meaningfully at John with a woebegone expression. "Ness has asked if I can take her exploring... I would love to show her around before she leaves and the forecast is rain for the next couple of days... you may not find the idea of Ness leaving us disappointing... but as you know I feel the disappointment keenly."

John paused with a forkful of sausage and egg hanging in mid-air... maybe Ewan could be trusted... then again maybe not... he'd let him go on his picnic... he would take the opportunity to call in without fear of being overheard. He had to safeguard himself; he would not take responsibility for Ewan's behaviour any longer... he could just voice his fears, let them take it from there. If Ewan's crimes were discovered, if it came out who he worked for... no matter what denials Moscow made the damage would be done... plans that had taken fifteen years of hard work... millions of pounds had been spent in securing allies from all sections of the community; the rich and the famous, the powerful and influential and not forgetting the common man, without whom no organised riot would have ever been possible. To come this close to success and then be thwarted at the last because of a careless blood thirsty serial killer... well it wouldn't be good for him especially... yes, he was calling Ewan in. John swallowed his mouthful.

"I don't see why not... if you work through until 1pm you can make the time up tomorrow."

"Thank you Sir John... I'll go and ask about the picnic now."

Ness went straight out the front and lit a cigarette. She congratulated herself on a quick recovery in there, but kicked herself for her stupidity... Flake was by no means senseless and to treat him as such would be sheer folly... she thought she had the upper hand... she had relaxed too easily into her part and it had nearly been her downfall. She would have to find Mark and tell him what was happening today... somehow.

Walking the back way into the kitchen, Ness opened the door to be met by gales of laughter. Mark, Agnes and the cook were seated round the table drinking tea. Agnes actually had tears rolling down her cheeks the cook was pink in the face, clutching at her stomach begging Mark to stop.

"Ach yer a cheeky wee monkey... the poor girl."

"It was meant as a compliment," Mark looked up as Ness entered. Agnes snorted into her cup. It was the first time Ness had seen Agnes laugh... she'd never so much as cracked a smile before the change it made to her was remarkable... she looked about ten years younger.

"Ah, Miss Gordon... I was just telling the ladies that I did the gentlemanly thing last night when I found you in the lane and escorted you home," his eyes flashed mischievously.

"If you hadn't had my bike to prop yourself up with you wouldn't have made it back here! Would it be possible for you to make Ewan and myself a picnic lunch?" Ness asked the cook. "It's such a lovely day he's offered to show me around the hills... I can do it if you're busy."

"Och away with ye lass, it's nay bother... and don't you mind that wee scoundrel; if ye ask me he fancies ye rotten. What time would you be needing the food, Miss?"

"One o' clock, thank you," Ness shot a look at Mark as she left, hoping he understood.

"Tch! I don't like the idea of that girl being alone with Ewan."

"Vera!" Admonished Agnes, shooting a meaningful look at Mark's bent head.

"I can have my opinions and like it or lump it I don't like him... he fair gives me the collywobbles... you know me, Agnes, I've never said a wrong word about an employer... but why Sir John gives that man the time of day is nobody's business," she began to fill the sink with hot suds, splashing crockery into the bowl. "You tell me why Sir John had the kitchen entrance to the back cellar locked and bolted... gave Ewan the space to work in, he told me... what about my poor old legs I told him... he'd fetch me anything I needed he says... I tell ye the man is up to nay good." She turned, waving a soapy spoon at Mark and Agnes. "Do you remember the snow storms in January, Agnes?" Not waiting for a reply, she continued. "I was cooking for a small house party and by the time I was ready to leave, the snow was knee deep and you couldn't see the hand in front of yer face... so I stoked up the fire, made myself a bite of super and settled down in yon armchair with a blanket." Mark looked to where Vera was pointing. A large squashy armchair sat in front of the fire, its back pushed to the wall. Just visible was the top of a small door. Vera put down the spoon and thrust her red hands back into the suds, triumphantly brandishing a juice jug in mid-air she continued in a low voice. "I woke up in the wee hours and couldn't remember where I was at first... I was about to nod off again when I heard it..." she paused for effect eyeing the others dramatically, "A screaming like I'd never heard the likes of afore... then him laughing and laughing... I got up and pushed the chair tight against the wall... didn't want him creeping up here... it went quiet... then, footsteps... banging and dragging... I heard Sir John shouting, then, silence." The juice jug was put on the drainer as Vera's soapy hands landed on plump hips. She had come to the climax of her story. "I heard the front door go and I crept out into the hall... what da ye think I seen?" Not waiting for an answer she carried on: "They were bundling someone wrapped in a blanket into the back of the car and they drove off... I went straight to Sir John in the morning and told him straight that I was not working in a house with such goings on... and he told me that Ewan had played a childish trick on his lady friend. Scared her stupid by telling her the cellar was haunted, then the idiot man crept up on her in the dark. She panicked and screaming her head off, had run straight into a low beam... Ewan apparently hadn't realised she had knocked herself out... as soon as he did he fetched Sir John and they took her to the hospital in town..." Wagging her finger at Mark she carried on, "Any man that can scare a girl half to death like that and think it funny is no man in my book!" Turning back to the sink she immersed herself in the rest of the washing up in an outraged silence.

Mark couldn't believe that a witness had appeared, genie-like, to substantiate the evidence Ness had found. Not only that, but there was a back way into the cellar... poor Vera. When she found out what she had actually overheard was the sadistic killing of a young woman she'd have a fit... then again... once she'd got over the shock, the telling of such a tale would hold her in high regard in the village for generations... the invites for tea would be endless... yes she'd recover without doubt. He checked his watch.

153

"Hell, is that the time? I'd better get back to work... thanks for breakfast ladies." He left the kitchen and walked around the grounds until he had found a spot where he couldn't be seen and couldn't be overheard. He pulled his phone from his pocket and dialled.

"Mate... she's off at one with him... you gonna pick up the tracker or you want me too?"

"I'll do it... he can't tell me to bugger off back to work if I get too close."

"Fair enough... we have a witness and a back door."

"What... no shit?"

"No shit... cook stayed over one night. Back door is in kitchen. She overheard him playing and what's more, saw the disposal. She doesn't realise it... she swallowed John's story but she's the goods all right. The net is closing in mate."

"Good. I'll call it in... keep me posted," Kalum hung up and called the chief.

"Sir,"

"Just a moment," Kalum could hear murmured voices and a door closing. The chief was taking no chances; he was convinced he had a mole in his department. He didn't want anyone knowing of their current op.

"Go ahead."

"We have a witness... evidence that the girl was held there, at least, and a back door to the cellar... Mark's going to check it out and see if he can get in tonight."

"And Ness?"

"She found the evidence, Sir. Brought it straight to us... she's going out with Flake this afternoon; I'm tailing."

"How long till it's wrapped up?"

"I reckon all done within next 48 hours."

"Good. I'm travelling up tomorrow... I hear the fishing's good."

"Look forward to seeing you Sir."

The chief hung up.

Tapping his pen on the desk he waited. Two minutes later the door opened and his secretary walked in carrying a coffee tray. Depositing it on his desk she asked if he wanted anything else.

"No, thank you... I think you've probably done quite enough..." he watched as her face flushed an angry red. "In fact, I think it's high time you left my department." He reached into a drawer and pulled out a file. "Sit down."

She sat opposite Ian. Her hands were shaking. She sat on them and tried to look him in the eye. He watched her bluntly in silence, waiting for her to speak.

Knowing when someone was up to no good was a hell of a lot different than having the evidence to back up the theory, he found the best policy was to infer wrongdoing, look like you had a glut of evidence to back it up and wait for the miscreant to confess... he didn't have to wait long. With her eyes darting from the floor to the file and back again the young secretary spluttered it all out: she was at a party, got drunk and loud. She had told whomever would listen who she worked for... a newspaper editor called Phil had offered her money in exchange for classified information... anything that could call security into question. She had agreed. The next day when she sobered up she had called him and said she had made a mistake, but he had threatened her... do as he asked or he would destroy her... she would be splashed across the tabloids... a messed up rich girl partying hard. He had photos of her half naked snorting coke... if he published it, she could kiss goodbye to her career. And it wouldn't stop there. He also had evidence her alcoholic mother was a regular visitor to a young male prostitute, he had some very unflattering and damming footage of them together on several occasions... her father may have to step down from the bar... the family's name and status would be smashed beyond repair. She had no choice and had agreed to do as he wanted but hadn't passed anything on, saying she hadn't been able to find anything. Head bent she sat whilst tears fell down her face. Ian ignored the tears.

He pushed the phone over to her. "Pull yourself together and call him. Tell him you have the information and get him to meet you in the café opposite…" he looked at his watch, "in one hour. Tell him you want everything he has on you and your mother or it's no deal."

She dialled, Ian put the phone on speaker and sat back listening. Fanshaw sounded naturally nervous; her whispered words were convincing… Phil was a grasping narcissistic asshole, his silky sly speech promising to hand over the evidence once he had the goods and that he wouldn't bother her again was a pile of fucking crap… Ian knew it. He'd be willing to bet as soon as the wanker got what he wanted he'd publish his dirty little story and get a kick watching the family crumble. He didn't doubt the video on Fanshaw's mum. It was a lucrative blackmail business in the shoddier run brothels… when Fanshaw turned up pissed at the same party he must have thought all his Christmas and birthday wishes had come at once.

Ian put a call through to a strictly private number at Scotland Yard. "I need a favour."

Forty minutes later a suited man with a briefcase stood on the pavement in front of the café and a taxi pulled in. The man in the smart suit stepped forward as the taxi door opened. Phil's head emerged briefly, his hand on the door handle. The man's hand also reached for the handle and briefly touched Phil's. He slumped back into the seat.

The man pushed him roughly to one side, jumped in beside him and the taxi sped off. Ian smiled. Phil was out of the picture; he would be made to call his office when he woke up and tell them he was following up an important story, and that he would call again in a few days. Before then, evidence would emerge of Phil's shady goings on, his repeated blackmail attempts to fabricate stories and that would be that... Fanshaw was on her way to be de-briefed; she could no longer be trusted. Her position in the establishment would have to be reassessed.

He liked leaving his office ship-shape when he went anywhere. Picking up the file he had used against the girl, he flicked it open... brochures of happy tourists enjoying a cruise in bright sunshine atop a crystal blue ocean produced a grin from ear to ear. His wife would be flabbergasted... she had put up with a lot over the years, him, his job and the compulsory, mostly unwelcome, complications it had brought to her life... this was his thank you for sticking by him. A retirement gift they could both enjoy... but not yet. He had an afternoon flight to Scotland to catch and a promise made twenty years ago to live up to.

Chapter Twelve

Give me the liberty to know, to utter, and to argue freely according to conscience, above all liberties.

– John Milton

Mark, driving the ride on mower, could see Ness as she followed behind Ewan who wore the backpack holding the picnic food. The path led through the back of the grounds and over the low stone wall that surrounded the land to the rear of the house.

Switching off the engine, Mark drank deeply from a cold water bottle. Shading his eyes from the sun, he watched as Ness followed Ewan over the style and carry on up the meandering path. Sheep skipped out of their way as they walked. Mark smiled and restarted the engine. Ness had ensured him that she could be seen for miles wearing a borrowed pillar box red straw hat that tied under her chin; she was like a warning beacon in the surrounding shades of soft green.

After a while the path took them through the edge of the pine forest as they disappeared from view. He messaged Kalum. 'No view. Heading north through pines. She has bright red hat on. Over to you now. Have you got her signal?'

Seconds later Kalum replied. 'Got her signal. Staying ahead. Contact you in one hour.'

Ness knew that Mark and her brother would be watching, she knew that they were both good at their jobs; they wouldn't let her down. The hat had been an extra precaution, just in case modern technology failed and if she needed to, she would scream and wave it. She looked at Ewan's back as he marched ahead, humming a tune. He seemed to have forgotten she was there. Patting her pocket, making sure her phone was safely in its depths, Ness glanced at her watch, 1.45pm. Where was he taking her?

"Ewan, is it much farther? I'm famished."

Turning around, he seemed surprised to find her at his heels.

"Not far... I promise, it's well worth the wait," and he carried on. Ness shrugged her shoulders and followed. The surrounding countryside was beautiful. All soft hills and green fields the scent of pine surrounded them. Under other circumstances, Ness would have loved the walk. It was pretty much evident that Ewan was a man on a mission; he was adamant that only one picnic spot would do. He assured her that the view was incredible and that the place held special meaning to him and he wanted to share it with Ness. Ness didn't think it was likely Ewan would try anything in the open country in the middle of the day, so murder wasn't his motive. So what was it?

The path forked two ways. Ewan led Ness down the left hand path they and emerged from the shade of the forest into open countryside. The hills grew tall above them, a mountain spring ran beside them. The sun caught the crystal clear water as it sped past, sending sparkles bouncing on the surface. Below them, stretched out like an artist's canvas, was the most incredible picture of country life; green fields, waving barley and flocks of sheep, way in the foreground stood the house. Ness stood with her hands on her hips,

"Wow Ewan, this is incredible!" There was no answer. Ness turned. Ewan stood right behind her. His hand fell to his side as she turned.

"Ready to eat?" He asked her, smiling. Bending to the rucksack, Ewan shook out a blanket laying it on the ground next to a grassy mound he patted it.

Ness sat, fishing in her pocket she brought out the packet of cigarettes and lit one.

"I'd love a cold drink first, if that's okay?" Ewan passed her a cold can of lemonade. She opened it and eagerly drank. Wiping her mouth with her free hand she put the empty can down next to her and took her phone out of her pocket. "I must get a photo of this view, it really is incredible. Well worth the walk," Ness dropped her cigarette stub into the empty can and standing up, took aim with the phone camera capturing the view around her.

"Sit down here, Ness, and I'll take a photo of you," Ness turned. Ewan was standing next to the mound. His usual pale cheeks were flushed, excitement rippled through his body his hands shook as he took the phone off Ness. He knelt and patted the grassy heap. Ness moved over to him.

"Yes that's right, sit down here," Ness sat on top of the heap. "No! That's not right... sit next to her... take that absurd hat off first, let your hair free," he stopped and looked expectantly at Ness unaware of what he had just given away. He was full of anticipation; an absurd excitement that made Ness want to vomit. Forcing a smile, she tentatively raised her hands to her head and undid the chin straps of her hat. Pulling it off, she took out the hair tie and combed her fingers through her hair, letting it cascade over her shoulders. Something was wrong. Her fingers worked through her hair until she found it again. A tuft of hair close to the back of her head... someone had cut a chunk of hair off leaving a rough stump! But how was that possible? She really felt like she was going to vomit now... for there was only one feasible answer for the missing hair and he was standing in front of her...She couldn't blow it now, she'd have to pull herself together and think of the young redhead, lying broken in the cold damp earth next to her... she shuddered, forced a grin and, looking up at Ewan, asked, "How's this?" She had sprawled herself next to the mound, one arm leaning across it with her chin resting on her upturned hand.

"That's perfect," Ewan snapped away.

Ness interrupted and, holding out her hand for her phone, laughed, "Now it's your turn," she scrambled to her feet. Ewan switched positions with her.

Ness raised the phone in front of her "I suppose it's so unspoilt up here because there's no road traffic." If she had to sit with the bastard and play nice she was going to get some fucking information out of the shit... how the hell did they get a body up here? Even though the girl had been small she would have been a dead weight and it would have been pitch black.

"Oh, there is a road... for farm vehicles mostly... you can't see it the way we came but it comes out just above us behind the stone wall there," Ewan pointed behind them and Ness looked. She could see the wall but not the road behind, something glinting between rocks and bushes about one hundred yards above them caught her eye. Her brother was close by.

She took a deep breath in, let it out slowly and, tucking the phone back into her pocket, smiled at Ewan. "I'm famished. Let's eat."

Engaging in conversation with a mass murderer whilst sitting by his last victim knowing he has you marked as his next is no easy task. Knowing that her brother was just above them watching made the task a little easier. She had mentally gone through a list as they were walking. First she wanted to know what Sir John, Ewan and the soviets were planning... it was something big, what with all those communications... lists had to be for something extreme. Anything she could get would be helpful. Then she wanted to know about Ewan's past... the where, when, why, and how a man turned into a bloodthirsty sadistic executioner... and how the hell did you get a job as chief torturer? Did you answer an ad? *Contract torturer required. Please provide cover letter, full CV, and samples of your work to*... to where? Ness bit into a large egg and cress roll aware that Ewan was watching her closely. She swallowed and took another big bite. It wasn't until she had finished her roll and eaten a slice of ham and egg pie, drank another lemonade that she dared herself to speak.

"Are you from Scotland Ewan? You don't have an accent," Ness reached for an apple, shining it on her shirt as she waited for him to speak.

"No... originally I'm from St Petersburg. I came here about twenty years ago."

"Really? I would never have guessed... you don't sound Russian. I suppose when you go back home to visit family you sound Russian."

Ewan looked at her quizzically... she was asking a lot of questions. Still, it didn't really matter. It's not as if she would be around much longer to tell anyone.

"I have no family. My mother died when I was twelve and I grew up in a state orphanage. It wasn't pleasant... my potential was realised and I was offered a job. I took it, and left."

"I'm so sorry Ewan," she even managed to look it. "That must have been hard for you... is it too much to ask how she died?" Ness held her breath. Had she gone too far?

"She was a prostitute. Someone hacked her to death one night; her and her unborn bastard. They were no loss," Ness leaned over and patted his hand. He looked at her quizzically, his eyes were a little glazed as he muttered "It was my first one... you always remember your first."

Ness drew in a sharp breath. His first one... he had killed his mother and her unborn child... what had he done in the orphanage for his potential to be realised? "Have another roll," Ness passed him a roll before carrying on. "Ewan's not a very Russian name, did you change it when you moved?"

"I was named after my father. He disappeared when my mother found out she was pregnant. He was British," Ewan spat out the word British Ness changed the subject; she could trace the orphanage. There can't have been many kids called Ewan who slaughtered their mother and sibling. She would find someone who would be willing to talk about the boy who was picked for his natural skills in butchery... who had honed those skills... offered him a job... put his particular skills to use for them.

'It must be interesting working for Sir John... all those lovely old books."

"It has its moments," He looked shrewdly at Ness "Its compensations."

"I suppose there's a fair bit of travelling involved."

"Yes... yes there is... we have a big trip planned in a fortnight," Ewan smiled a lazy, greedy smile, his eyes were far away on some bright longed for event. "Two weeks today. Everything is set, the players are all on the board... Times are changing, Ness... but of course you won't be here to see them," he looked at the grassy mound next to him and stroked the length of it. "I'll visit and tell you all about it."

Ness shivered. It was time to go. She forced a laugh. "I don't have a clue what you're talking about, Ewan, but it sounds exciting! I'll give you my address when I leave," he looked at her, confused, then he tittered, covering his mouth with his hand.

"Oh, of course... yes, your address... how would I find you without it? Shall we pack up?"

Ness agreed and handed Ewan empty containers to go back into the rucksack. She kept her eyes down and on the task in hand. The guy had lost the plot... he was a raving loony. Did his Moscow bosses know they had a loose cannon? Obviously not, since he was still breathing.

Lighting a cigarette while she had a last look at the view, Ness jumped as she heard her name being called. "Oi! Ness!" she turned to see Kalum heading down towards them. He waved, she waved back. She was actually relived to see him; he could walk back with them. Ewan did not look happy as Kalum held out his hand to him, "You must be Ewan... I'm Kalum, Max's husband... it is beautiful up here."

"We were just heading back down," Ewan's voice was clipped.

"Great, I'll walk back with you... lead on."

All the way back down the hill Kalum kept up a steady stream of polite, safe conversation. By the time they reached the style leading to the house Ewan had become quite chatty, offering Kalum and Max a dinner invitation for the following evening. He and Sir John had to go out again tonight but were both free tomorrow. Kalum readily accepted, saying how thrilled Max would be, he hoped they wouldn't mind her looking around the place and taking some notes for her book. Kalum checked his watch.

"It should be safe to go back now... Max kicked me out this morning; said it was impossible to work with me hanging around, I've been walking for hours!"

"Ewan!" Sir John emerged from the front door "We have to leave," he turned to Kalum and Ness,

"Forgive me if I appear rude... I have an evening meeting to attend and due to an unfortunate turn of events the venue has changed."

"Nothing too serious I hope," asked Ness.

"No... just inconvenient... a double booking I believe."

"Give me the rucksack, Ewan and I'll take it into the kitchen... Kalum do you think Max will mind if I cycle down later? I'll be leaving in a couple of days and since Sir John and Ewan will be out, it'd be good to spend more time with Max. Only if she's finished for the day," she looked at John and Ewan, "Max is lovely, but a hellish temper if you interrupt whilst she's working."

"I'm sure she'd love to see you Ness, why don't you give her a call," Ness laughed.

"Yeah and get in trouble instead of you for interrupting her... I'll get rid of this and then give her a call... maybe see you later," Ness waved a goodbye walking round to the kitchen. She heard Ewan remind Kalum of the dinner invitation for 7pm the following evening then the slamming of two car doors and the hum of the engine as the car moved off down the driveway.

The kitchen was empty. Ness opened the rucksack and taking a tissue lifted out a half-eaten apple dropping it into a sandwich bag she pressed it closed. It couldn't hurt to have a DNA sample and possibly a set of his prints from her mobile she'd been very careful handling it after he took his photos. She finished clearing up the picnic things and left a note for Agnes saying she wouldn't be home for dinner, she'd get a takeout and have it with Max.

Ness went up to her room, washed her face and hands, collected her handbag, dropping the sandwich bag containing the half apple into it before heading back downstairs.

The house was eerily silent. She hadn't met anyone since she'd returned. Standing at the top of the stairs Ness listened... nothing. As she reached the bottom a door shut quietly. Sure it had come from the kitchen, Ness made her way there. Standing outside of the door she listened; there was definitely someone there. Pushing the door open quickly she stepped into the kitchen. Agnes swung around with Ness' note in her hand.

"Miss Gordon... it's just as well you'll not be in for dinner," Agnes pointed to the modern Aga. "The cooker's broken... Mark has had the thing in bits all afternoon but has had to order a part in from the suppliers... it'll be here first thing in the morning."

"Oh dear...what about your dinner Agnes?"

"I'll warm something in the microwave... will you be late back?"

"Oh I'm not sure I'll ring you," Ness's mobile rung; it was Max.

"Ness get down here double quick... you'll be staying the night."

"Talk of the devil Max... I'd love too, see you in twenty minutes," She smiled at Agnes "It looks like I won't be back tonight, Max wants me to stay... I'll just grab some clothes and I'll see you in the morning Agnes."

Max had sounded serious, something was wrong; had someone's cover been blown? She'd soon find out. Ness fetched the bicycle and lighting a cigarette, peddled off down the driveway. At least she knew the way now.

Peddling down the lane Ness had to admit that she more than happy not to be staying in Dracula's castle tonight... would I have been so eager if it had been Kalum issuing the order? She chuckled... definitely not. Mark? No to that, too... although she would have answered his summons, in her own time. Hell, who was she trying to kid? She would have peddled down bloody quick whoever had phoned... this wasn't about her any more, this was about justice for a young runaway who had no one at her back, unlike Ness who had had more support over the years than she was aware of at the time.

Parking her bike outside the house she knocked on the door. Max opened it, hugged her and ushered her in before closing the door behind them.

"We're in the kitchen Ness, go through," Ness walked into the kitchen ready to give a cheery hello and stopped dead. Kalum and Mark were standing by the table and both wore expressions of fury mingled with horror. Ness raised her hands in mock surrender.

"Whoa! Whatever it was, I didn't do it... I have abided by all rules and once again come bearing gifts," she put her bag on the table and sat down looking from Kalum to Mark. "Well...what's wrong?"

Max put a mug of coffee down in front of Ness and pushed an ashtray towards her before sitting down herself and lighting up a cigarette. "I suggest Ness tells us what she has for us before we begin," Ness looked up quickly at Max. Whatever it was, it was serious.

Ness placed the bag with apple on the table and next to it her phone. "I didn't know if you had Flake's DNA; this is his apple." She pushed it further onto the table. "My phone has his prints on it, I'm not sure if that's useful or not, but I thought it may help find other victims of his." She paused. "Also on my phone are several photos of the place he buried his last victim, there is a road you can drive almost straight to the spot... and it can be done unseen at night," this was the bit she wasn't looking forward too. She didn't want to tell them that someone had cut rather a large chunk of her hair off and she didn't have a clue how it had been done... but they would have to know. "Em... also..." Her hand fluttered to her head, feeling for the rough stump of hair. "Um..." She looked from her brother to Mark. Why the hell did they both look so angry? Maybe she'd keep quiet. Max's hand covered hers and squeezed gently. "They're not angry with you Ness."

Ness lit another cigarette and without looking at either man announced "Someone has cut my hair and I don't know how or when." She drained her coffee cup.

Chapter Thirteen

This is not the end. It is not even the beginning of the end. But it is, perhaps, the end of the beginning

– Winston Churchill

Kalum exchanged a look with Mark. "We know."

Hell this was going to be hard. Max had said he wasn't angry with Ness but he was, they both were. She had been told to lock her door, keep herself safe, but she hadn't. Granted, Ness couldn't have known Flake had positioned cameras around her room. Couldn't have foreseen that he would creep into her room in the dead of night and do... and do that to her. For fuck's sake after everything they had told her... shown her... he felt sick... the bastard had taken his mother. Watching those same vile hands touch his sister was too much. She could bloody well watch it herself. Then they'd show her what else Mark found.

He held his hand out to Mark and snapped his fingers. "Give it to me."

"Mate, are you sure? Maybe you should just explain."

"I said give it to me. Now Mark."

"Your funeral," he passed a USB stick to Kalum who loaded it into the side of a laptop sitting on the table then he pressed play. "Watch closely, Ness. The mystery of your missing hair is about to be explained."

Ness looked from her brother to Mark. What the fuck was going on? She looked back at the screen and her eyes widened in shock. She covered her mouth with shaking hands as she watched Flake walking to the side of her bed and cut her hair. She wanted to vomit as he entered the tip of the blade into her body, she blanched as she watched him spit on her vagina and recoiled at his pleasure as he stood, head to one side watching his spit leave a glistening trail down her soft flesh. The screen went blank. Ness sat motionless for moments then rushed to her feet, sending the chair flying. She raced upstairs to the bathroom and vomited.

When she had finished Ness stayed kneeling on the bathroom floor. Stupid, stupid cow, you're a fucking fool, Ness Gordon... it's no bloody wonder they're angry with you... lock yourself in, keep safe... you can't even manage that... stupid, stupid cow. Ness slapped herself on the forehead with the palm of her hand as she continued to scold herself. A cough at the door made her look up. Mark stood in the doorway with a glass of water she flushed crimson to the roots of her hair and groaned. "Great, that's all I fucking need."

"Aw, come on Ness... we all make mistakes, yours just seem to be more... um, impressive than most," he knelt down by the side of her and passed her the glass. "Drink up. Kalum wants you back downstairs." He watched her raise the glass to her lips, Mark didn't agree with Kalum on this, but it was his decision, his sister. When Kalum said Ness was finished, he was pulling her out and Mark had to comply... which was fine. He didn't want her near Flake any longer than necessary, but to drug her and lock her up... plus he had a nagging suspicion that the whole operation would go a lot smoother with Ness' help... but it wasn't his call.

"Mark...I can manage a glass of water by myself... if you don't mind, a little privacy please."

"Oh, yeah... right... em... sorry Ness," he gave her shoulder a squeeze and went back down stairs.

Something was wrong. Mark was sympathetic. Kind even, his anger gone. Ness looked closely at the glass of water. It looked like water, she sniffed it, no obvious smell...would her brother drug her to get her out of the way? Probably... would she go without a fight? Like hell she would. Ness tipped the water down the loo and flushed. Standing up, she turned the tap on and splashed her face before rinsing her mouth out, then she washed the glass, rinsed it again then filling it a quarter full headed back downstairs. As she entered the kitchen three concerned faces turned to her. Ness cleared her throat, set the glass on the table and opening a new pack of cigarettes from her bag and lit one. She looked at their faces. All of them threw occasional unguarded looks that flickered between the glass and herself. So she was right.

"Look guys… I'm sorry if you feel I let you down. I was sure I locked the door. If I didn't, then what happened was my own fault. I presume there is other footage of me and I would ask that you destroy it… all of it. As you can imagine it's extremely embarrassing. Max, I could murder a coffee if there's one going." She watched as Max exchanged a look with Kalum. He gave an almost unperceivable shake of his head. "There is more I have to tell you. Flake has reserved a spot for me next to the grave in the photo. I think he means to take me the morning after I finish work, which is the day after tomorrow," she paused for effect. "I suggest we use what we know to our full advantage… make it work for us, so to speak. I take it from what we have all just watched that Mark has found a way into Flake's den; I may also have found the number code. Two weeks from today something is planned. I don't know what but I think it has something to do with the correspondence they have been receiving; I got the impression it will be colossal, involve a lot of people. Flake is very excited for the day to arrive… he seems to expect a shift of power; he indicated after the event he would be top dog, so it's a takeover of some sort... I can try and find out more," she looked up at the others.

Kalum was scrutinising Ness closely. The sedative should have taken effect by now.

Ness tapped the glass. "Kalum I'm not a fool...I didn't drink it," she sat back and waited for hell to explode over her head, but the silence in the room spoke for itself. Ness felt her temper rising and that wouldn't do if she were to argue her case and win, she looked at Max. "Do I get a coffee now? Probably better if I make it myself... safer for my health that way."

Ness moved across the kitchen, emptied, rinsed and refilled the kettle before switching it on and spooning coffee into the pot. She sat back down at the table putting the tray with the coffee, four mugs, milk and sugar onto the table. Nobody had spoken. "Sorry if I was sharp with you Max... I know it was his decision. So Kalum... do I get an explanation or are you going to try and lock me up now?" She leant forward... "I won't go quietly and I think I have the right to know what else he found out," She thumbed Mark's direction, "before you make your final decision." Mark sat down next to her and poured coffee into four mugs. Ness inched her chair away from him.

Kalum sat down opposite Ness, leaning back in the chair, stretching his legs out under the table. He folded his arms across his chest, narrowed his eyes and frowned at her. Mark raised an eyebrow at him,

Kalum nodded. "Show her... let's see if she's still keen after this."

Mark plugged his phone into the laptop and when it had loaded swung it round so it faced Ness.

"I did get into the cellar; I broke the cooker so I could get the place to myself. I'll fix it tomorrow. Be warned Ness... what you are about to see is not for the squeamish..." he pressed slide show. Picture after picture flashed past Ness. The big gleaming steal table taking centre stage on a raised platform, its intricate pulley system coiled above it. The straps used to secure one's body to the table at the head, waist, wrists and legs. The operating room style lighting and cabinets filled with knives, scalpels, saws, clamps and long sharp hooks and steel pliers of various sizes. There were cameras positioned around the table, a hose curled up next to a stainless steel sink and bottles of hospital grade disinfectant stood in the cupboard beneath it. A red curtained cabinet; then the curtains were open to reveal row after row of varying shades and lengths of red hair each with a name tape below it and in a drawer, DVD cases with names corresponding to the hair pieces.

"Stop for a second," Ness looked at Kalum. "Why the fixation with wigs?" Mark spoke.

"They're not wigs Ness... the last barbaric act he completes is to scalp her. He keeps them as trophies." Mark paused and looked to Kalum.

"Show her," Kalum growled in reply

Ness looked back at the screen as the next picture flicked into view. It was a wig stand like the others, it had no occupant as yet but the name tape stuck to the base clearly showed who it was reserved for. Ness swallowed and reached for a smoke before she spoke. She wanted to be bloody sure she sounded fearless and confident.

"We knew he was after me, that's why you agreed to let me help. We also knew what he did to the poor bitches he got hold of. Okay, so we didn't know about the scalps, but we did know he had a weakness bordering on an obsession with red hair and we knew about the DVDs. The only difference this makes is we now have solid proof and a way into the cellar. We know he wants me and we know where he will put me. We know where he buried his last, with John's help and a witness that saw them load her into the car… I know if I end up in that cellar you will get me out. The only place I definitely don't want to end up is next to that poor little bitch on the hill," Ness sat back in her chair and waited. She'd said her piece, but she was not going to go quietly if her brother insisted she stay out of it from now on. She looked from one face to the next, finishing up with Kalum who still looked likely to spring on her and use brute force if necessary. It was Max who broke the silence. "I don't know about you lot, but I'm famished. Who's for takeout?" Kalum glowered, Mark gave the thumbs up and Ness smiled at Max.

"That is the best suggestion I've heard all afternoon, yes please, Max."

Kalum's phone rang he picked up the call, walking into the other room with it. Ness strained to hear from the kitchen.

"Sir... London, Glasgow and Manchester... Ness has a date that could prove conclusive... two weeks today country wide... that could explain the hurry this afternoon... fits in Sir... okay see you then... yes, Sir, I'll tell her."

Kalum appeared in the doorway. "The chief says well done Ness, the date you gave ties in with the intelligence he received this morning. The net is closing in on them, our job is to get Flake... The chief will be here himself later this evening and we'll go through the final phase then." He looked at Ness, guessing her thoughts. "It's my call, Ness; my decision if you carry on or not, appealing to the chief to override me won't work. Understand?" Ness nodded. "Good." He sat down as the doorbell rang. Max answered, coming back into the kitchen a couple of minutes later with two large bags of takeout. She set the containers on the table, grabbed cutlery and sat down.

Mark grabbed the nearest container, opened the lid, took a fork from the pile on the table and started cramming the food into his mouth. He stopped to look at Ness, "It's not poisoned Ness." He opened another container, shoved a forkful of noodles into his mouth, chewed and swallowed before passing her the container. "See? Just food."

Silence surrounded the table as they ate. Ness made more coffee while Kalum and Mark picked the containers clean. When she judged it safe, Ness asked Kalum the question burning her thoughts.

"Kal, umm... can I stay... please?" He had already decided she should carry on. He couldn't deny she had brought valuable intelligence to the table and if he was brutally honest the operation would go smoother with her on board. He sat back in his chair, looked at Mark and Max, who both nodded their approval.

"You stay, but no more snooping on your own Ness... this is going to be a tight operation and we need to know where you are going to be at all times." He leaned forward, "And where you will be is where we tell you to be... you know what Flake's capable of. We can't risk him taking you before we're in place... understand?"

"Yes Kalum," she beamed at him, "thank you," Mark chuckled

"That's the second time I've heard someone say thank you for allowing them to be placed in immediate danger. You're a chip off the old block, Ness."

"Mark," Kalum growled

"Sorry, mate."

There was a knock at the back door. Mark slipped into the other room, Kalum strode over to the door and swung it open. Standing back he let someone enter; Ness looked up. A man in his sixties stood in the kitchen. Carrying fishing gear, he was dressed in jeans, wellington boots and a fleece lined weather proof jacket. He dumped his gear on the floor, crossed to the table and sat down. His was a commanding presence with sharp, intelligent, crystal blue eyes. He scanned the others at the table pausing to smile at Max.

"It's good to see you Max... boys okay?"

"Fine, Sir. How's the office?"

"Still standing," his eye fell on Ness. "You behaving yourself?" She flushed and met him eye for eye before replying, "You know exactly what I've been doing."

Ian nodded. "I guess I do... Kalum letting you stay on board?" She nodded. "Good," he turned to Kalum. "You told her yet?"

"No, Sir... I didn't think it necessary."

Ian looked at Kalum with sympathy. "There's never going to be a right time Kalum. I've been talking to psych; if she goes in there and those memories surface she may be left vulnerable, unable to protect herself, the consequences may be far reaching and long lived. Understand?"

"Yes, Sir," Max squeezed his arm "Let the Chief tell it, Kalum," He nodded.

Ness looked from one to the other... what the fuck was going on now?

The chief lit a cigarette, ignoring the harsh tut from Max. He took a deep drag and spoke, letting the smoke out in small puffs.

"Twenty years ago I worked with your mother. She was one of the best operatives we had. She trained Max in the field, was loyal to her country and its citizens... a fierce adversary... loving mum and loyal friend..." he took another drag. "She was befriended by a foreign agent trying to get crucial information back to her handler in Moscow. Your mum, being no fool knew what this woman was up to and didn't give anything away. The agent's handler got tired of waiting and sent in a new recruit whose speciality was loosening tongues." He tapped the ash off his cigarette and leant forward toward Ness. "Flake was, and is, his name. His art wasn't as fine-tuned as it is now; in those early days he was untidy. Your brother was first on the scene what he found was hard for a young man to handle... he called us and covered your mum up... when we arrived Kalum was holding her. She managed to tell me what had happened... she was desperate to tell us she had hidden you, desperate to keep you safe from him. She died in Kalum's arms and he found you hidden in a kitchen cupboard... you had your hands pressed tight to your eyes. Your mum must have given you strict

183

instructions to follow: don't look, don't speak, don't make a sound... you clung on so tight to him and refused to let go. You didn't speak for a fortnight and when you did, you had no recollection of that night... Kalum, determined to hunt the bastard down, joined us and became your protector... your only family. Problem is, he spoilt you rotten... showered you with love and gifts but no discipline," the chief finished. All eyes turned to Ness.

She lit a cigarette, drew in a deep drag, exhaled and looked at her brother. "Kalum... I'm so sorry... I... I really don't know what to say... I don't remember it at all... you carried this for all these years, alone."

"Not alone Ness, never alone... the Chief was mum's friend. He and Max have watched out for both of us. We couldn't tell you when you were younger, too much was at risk and then, well, you grew up and priorities had to change," Ness walked over to her brother threw her arms around his neck and hugged him hard.

"I'm sorry for being a bitch, Kal. Thank you... for everything," she turned to Ian and Max "I really don't know what to say... sorry... thank you," Max leant over and patted her hand. "It's all right, Ness. Let's just get the job done so we can all move on."

Ness sat back in her chair. She didn't know which emotion to harness and hold onto. They were all there, pulsing through her veins beating at her temples. Sorrow, guilt, anger. Their mum, the woman she believed had callously abandoned them, leaving the responsibility of her upbringing to Kalum. He had been twenty, ancient to a six year old, but really little more than a boy himself. When he should have been out partying, he was struggling with a grief and horror she couldn't imagine, let alone her total selfishness. Her mum's last words as Kalum had cradled her bloodied broken body were to look after Ness and to kill the evil bastard who wrecked their little family. Harness the anger. She nodded to herself, stubbed out her cigarette end and looked up to find Ian watching her with a perceptive eye. He raised an eyebrow in silent query and she nodded smiling back at him. "I'm glad you told me."

"Good. Now how much do you know about Flake?"

"I know he's losing it... rapidly... he's given me information without realising it. He thinks I won't be around to cause trouble."

Ian interrupted: "What information?"

"His first victims were his own mother and unborn sibling, his father is British. According to Flake he left them when his mum found out she was expecting. He grew up in a state orphanage in St Petersburg where his talents were quickly realised and he was taken for training by..." Ness paused. "...I don't know who, but I would guess from what he said a government agency. He took me to where he buried his last corpse and he showed me where I would lay by her side with delight. I think he felt I should feel honoured. He gave me the date of two weeks today, saying it was a shame I would miss it, but that he would visit me and tell me what happened." Ness shrugged "…I think Sir John knows Flake has little sanity left and is worried he will wreck the operation. Both John and Agnes know Flake is a loose cannon and I get the impression both of them are ready to shop him to Moscow." Ian nodded.

"It always pays to know your mark's psyche. Knowing what makes people tick, how their personality became them, can be incredibly useful… especially in an operation of this sort; where there is so much to lose: our country, our way of life; a united free Europe stands on the point of toppling into a dark chaos of the likes we truly haven't seen before. не мне gathers support in full view of the world, his armies march ever closer. Anybody believing his: "Russia is no threat" speech is a fool. Then we have ISIS, promising foreign fighters children to use, abuse and discard… hardly a surprise that their units are swollen with paedophiles willing to kill to feed their sadistic appetites. However unlikely, it is all connected… our priority is to secure Britain from within, take out Flake and shut down Sir John." He looked around the table. "And this is how it will happen."

Chapter Fourteen

To have begun is half the job: be bold and be sensible.

– *Horace*

Sir John slowed and stopped the car at a set of traffic lights as they made the change from amber to red. The weather forecast had been right; a steady light drizzle of rain drummed on the car roof as large dark storm clouds formed above and a distant rumble of thunder echoed through the night.

Stealing a sideways glance at Ewan, John frowned. The situation was worrying, worrying enough to have contacted Moscow this afternoon. He went back to studying the traffic lights.

The conversation hadn't been accommodating; he had explained Ewan was out of control, a liability to the whole operation. His blood lust had taken over any sanity that remained. He had emphasised Ewan's infatuation with the girl... told them of the other girl buried on the hillside and his expectation that Ness will join her within days if Ewan is not stopped. His fears that the operation would be foiled had fallen on deaf ears. They weren't prepared to listen and had made it plain that the success of the operation in the UK began and ended with John. There had been one proviso; if Ewan were discovered, if prosecution was likely and the media dug too deep, if there was any tangible evidence linking Ewan and his skills directly to Moscow, then Ewan's life would be terminated, his contract finished.

The lights changed and John moved off. Ewan was still staring ahead with a glassy eyed stare and an eerie grin. His hand drifted every few minutes to his pocket; he slipped it inside then would draw it out, patting the outside and smiling broadly before sliding back into contented apathy.

John turned the car down a small side street and pulled up in front of a Victorian terrace block, switching the engine off he got out of the car. Ewan hadn't moved. John leant in the open door.

"Time to go Ewan, everyone is waiting for us,"

Ewan came out of his reverie, "Yes... yes of course they are. Let's get it done and get home... lots to do... things to prepare," he left the car and walked ahead of John into the building's gloomy passageway. John followed Ewan up two flights of stairs and down a short corridor passing by thick wooden brown doors. Stopping outside number six, Ewan rapped sharply on the knocker and the door opened to reveal a small man of stocky build with a shaven head. He held the door open as the two men entered and closed it firmly behind them and followed down the tiled passage into a large, well lit room.

There was one other person in the room. He rose as John entered and moved forward reached out to shake his hand.

"Delighted to meet you at last, I have everything here." He triumphantly fluttered a piece of paper in John's face. "Security codes to all police stations in every town and city targeted, escape routes for the Palace, Downing Street and, of course, we have our people stationed inside... their cover is secure. Well, it would be; they've been in place for the last three years." He was full of joy, expectation. If he had been a dog John would have patted him. Instead he smiled and congratulated him. The man carried on talking, offering drinks which were declined. John almost felt sorry for him, the man and the thousands like him who had sworn to follow the cause to the bitter end, were, in reality, just tools. Tools meant to riot, loot, murder, cause as much chaos as possible. They thought they were leading a revolution. Idiots... a revolution against what? They lived in one of the most liberal democratic societies in the world, enjoyed an abundance of freedoms without suppression; yet they were still not satisfied. Convinced they were hard done by, owed more. They were owed nothing but wanted everything. The man talked on; none of it really mattered. The demonstrations would go ahead and they would rapidly escalate into riots, the rioters would attempt to get into the Palace and Downing Street without success. They would get into some of the police stations. But it wouldn't be a victory, not yet. When it was over, amid the smouldering ruins, allegations and blame, those carefully placed in positions of power would take over with the peoples blessing. An unstable Europe would witness a discombobulated Britain which in turn would give rise to their own rioting and subsequent power struggle. Britain and the USA would no longer be allies and the new order would sweep the globe. Taking over countries from the inside was a long thought out strategy and a lucrative business plan. This particular one had been in the making for the past ten years. John nodded and smiled at the man who was now talking him through a detailed map of the intended route. Poor bastard, if only he realised that he and several other agitators would end their lives on the route he was so eager to travel. Those that had direct contact with John, those who had received orders from Moscow would all die a swift death. Stabbing in these situations was the preferred method; it was quick and untraceable. No loose ends and if anything went wrong, there would be nothing to tie John or Moscow to the events. John reached out to shake the man's hand.

"Most satisfactory... I'll be in touch in the usual manner." Reaching into his jacket pocket, John pulled out a wad of used notes. "Expenses for the month... a little more than usual... a thank you for hard work," The two men beamed. The money would be spent quickly.

They were accompanied to the flat door, their hands wrung in iron grips. The door closed behind them as they made their way back down the corridor and out into the night.

The drive back was as silent as the drive up had been. John tried to engage Ewan in conversation but had quickly given up.

Ewan fingered the hair in his pocket, sliding the lock between each finger, enjoying the silkiness of it against his skin. He settled back in his seat, closing his eyes, envisioning Ness's naked vulnerable body... the flash of steel as the tip entered her... her musky scent on the blade... This was going to be his best work. He frowned. For the first time in his career he was seriously considering entering her himself. There had to be a first time for everything after all, yes why not? He would position her on her front, slightly raised and shackled. He would take her pussy whilst he gouged her arse with... with what? Not a blade, not yet... he mentally listed his tools. He wanted something thick. Substantial and long, it had to be long... he would have a look when he got home... watch the DVD again... yes, that's what he'd do. Pity she wasn't home tonight... no matter, she would watch it with him tomorrow night... he'd waited long enough.

The car turned into the driveway. "Thank goodness... we're back," Ewan turned to smile at John and noticed lights dancing on the hillside. "What's that... who's up there?" John heard the panic in his voice and knew it wasn't against discovery; he thought himself way above that. Quite simply, Ewan didn't want anyone touching his property: the girl's grave.

"Relax Ewan, it's probably just a scout camp. They asked for my permission last week and I gave it. Now, I am going to get myself a very large scotch and I'm off to bed, it's been a long day... I suggest you do the same."

Ewan stood watching the lights. He scowled. They had better leave the place as they found it. The scowl left his face as he remembered his plans for the night, whistling he made his way to the cellar.

***

The tent on the hillside was pitched over the grave. Inside, two men dug away the earth carefully, deliberately. A forensic pathologist stood by their side, camera at the ready, waiting until she was needed again. Outside, two more men stood guard. Lights hung around the incident tent, swinging in the wind. No one made a sound; voices carried far in the still nights and all were fully aware of what was at stake.

One of the diggers turned to the pathologist and gave her the thumbs up. She stepped forward, photographed the body from every angle, then handed over a plastic bag. The man filled it with a soil sample and handed it back. Between them they gently lifted the remains into a body bag. More photos were taken. The bag was sealed and smoothly carried to the van hidden from view amongst the pines.

Inside the tent, all the soil was carefully lifted back into the empty grave, the turf carefully removed before it was laid exactly as it had been, flowers and all. All traces of their activities were removed, the incident tent and lights were packed into the van. They drove off.

When they reached the main road one of the men pulled out a mobile and dialled.

"We have her, Sir... area fully photographed... soil samples in the bag...you wouldn't know we'd been there... heading back to London now."

"Good. Results are strictly for my eyes only. Call if there's a problem if not... wait for my call before acting," Ian hung up. Step one was complete; they had secured the evidence and retrieved the girl. He looked at Ness. Would she be strong enough to go through with tomorrow's strategy? He thought she was... Kalum, he knew, was still dubious, but that was only natural. Mark, unless he was very much mistaken had fallen for Ness hook line and sinker... he just hadn't realised it yet. Ian smiled... he'd met his own wife under similar circumstances. She was as head strong and as fiery as Ness… ah well he would just have to wait and see. He spoke to the table at large. "They have her."

A collective sigh stirred the table like a soft summer breeze. Kalum was the first to speak.

"Good, makes tomorrow's operation less… complicated…" He considered Ness with a hard stare. "You should get to bed." Ness had lit a cigarette. She felt a strange mix of sadness and joy. Sad for the girl's end, joy they had gotten her away from Flake. She looked up at her brother's eyes, full of suspicion.

"You'd better not be thinking of locking me in."

"I said you're in with us Ness… don't give me cause to change my mind."

"How do I know you're telling the truth?" Before Kalum could open his mouth to answer, Mark jumped in.

"Ness!" She took one look at Mark's steely dangerous eyes and stood up stubbing out her cigarette.

"Jesus, calm down… I'm going."

Ian raised an eyebrow at Kalum, he grinned in return they both looked at Mark who was watching Ness' retreating back with a half-smile. He looked up, caught them studying him and reddened. He spoke gruffly.

"Huhu... think I'll turn in as well... early start... busy day... um, see you all tomorrow." He left closing the back door softly behind him. Max looked at her watch. "2am... I think a few hours rest for all of us is a good idea."

Kalum lay in the lounge, staring at the ceiling. He didn't need to sleep, resting the body was enough. He thought about the next twenty four hours... twenty years he had waited for this and not for a single moment had he envisioned his sister's involvement in the plan. He had no doubts of her capability to cope with what lay ahead... she was strong willed, intelligent and had a knack for thinking on her feet. He would have to trust her as he expected her to trust him. He chuckled... I hope Mark knows what he's getting into.

***

Ness took a deep steadying breath and knocked on Sir John's study, opening the door at his muffled "Enter". She walked into the room. Ewan was gazing out of the window at the hillside, his hand busy in his pocket, Sir John was at his desk.

"Good morning Sir John... Ewan," smiling at them both, Ness headed for her own desk and the last sheaf of papers to be typed up.

"Morning, Miss Gordon, did you have a pleasant evening with your friends?"

"Yes thank you, Sir John. Max says they will be here a little after 5pm to look around, if that's okay with you? She's really looking forward to it."

"Yes... yes, of course. As am I."

Ewan came out of his trance and walked to stand at Ness's side. "Ness... as John and I are going to be busy tomorrow I have taken the liberty of booking you onto the sleeper to London tonight... I'll give you a lift to the station myself."

"Thank you, Ewan, how very considerate, what time should I be ready to leave?"

"The train leaves at seven forty." Ewan glanced at John. "I do hope your friends won't be disappointed but as the agar is still in pieces, Cook suggests a high tea instead of dinner." He paused to flick an imaginary piece of dust off his jacket. "Max can do her research, we can have a pleasant farewell tea and then I'll take you. Does that sound okay?"

"Lovely, thank you Ewan. I'll ring Max later... no, I'd better ring Kalum; don't want my head bitten off if she's busy!" Ness laughed and bent her head to her work. She didn't miss the pointed look of warning from John to Ewan, nor the smirk in return.

Ness typed on at top speed. The hours flew by, John remained at his desk. Ness suspected he was loath to leave her on her own with Ewan, who had settled himself in a chair directly behind her with a book, sporadically letting out small bursts of laughter, following each one with an apology for disturbing them both. Ness finished and checked her watch. It was one thirty.

"All done, Sir John, is there anything else you would like me to do for you? If not, I'll go and pack." John looked up from his desk.

"Thank you, Miss Gordon, you've done remarkably well; so quick. I'll see you for tea." He watched as Ness left the study. As soon as the door closed he turned on Ewan. "I told you, I don't want the girl harmed whilst she is in my employment," he glared at Ewan "... What do you think will happen when nobody has heard from her, when it's realised she never got on that train, that you were the last person to see her? Where do you think they will come knocking?" Ewan sniggered.

"I'll make sure she is capable of messaging her friends, telling them of her safe arrival in London and that she bumped into an old friend on the train who has persuaded her to stay for a few days... London can be a dangerous place for a woman travelling alone... as you know, anything can happen..." Ewan's cold blue eyes met John's... "You must allow me my little treat, John... my recreation. You have your books after all," he walked to the window, watching Ness talking on her phone and laughing. A slow cruel cold smile spread across his face as he watched her and thought of the tool he liberated from the dusty attic last night. An old weapon of iron, twelve inches long, rounded with sharp edged iron studs protruding from its length save a few inches left clear for the owner to wield its savagery. In a few hours he could trial its new purpose... what was it his mother used to tell him? Good things come to those who wait. He had waited and watched, dreamed of having Ness' flesh beneath his hands... he closed his eyes and imagined her naked on his table, at his mercy. Pulling the length of hair out of his pocket he held it to his face and inhaled her scent. John watched him with repulsion... he would not help him clean the mess up this time... in fact he didn't want to be in the same house while Ewan practised his vile art, whilst he enjoyed his... recreation.

Ness sat on the balcony outside her room with a strong pot of coffee. The packing was finished, Kalum had been called, all she had to do was wait. It was easier said than done. When she was busy, the cold fluttering feeling of dread vanished, but inactivity fed it. She was unable to sit in her room knowing it was watched and unwilling to seek refuge in the kitchen, afraid her eyes would slide too often towards the door to the cellar. She drained the coffee pot into her mug and glanced at her watch... four thirty. She'd wait another fifteen minutes before heading back downstairs. Leaning further back in the chair, Ness raised her face to the afternoon sunshine.

The trip had certainly been a surprising one. Arriving on Phil's instruction to get the dirt on Sir John, she had instead wandered unwittingly into a covert operation to save her country and catch a serial killer, had unmasked her brother as an intelligence agent, been taken hostage, had a gun pointed at her head by his roguish partner and discovered the truth about her mother's disappearance. She lit another cigarette. All things considered, not a bad week's work. It would make a great story. Pity most of it would remain untold... a promise was a promise. She would rather be in a locked room with an angry Mark than piss Ian off... Ian was somebody you crossed at your peril, besides she now knew what she owed the man and that deserved some loyalty.

Stubbing out her cigarette Ness stood, took a deep steadying breath and turned to head inside. She stopped. I wonder what happened to Phil... whatever it was, she would bet it wasn't a pleasant experience... you never know, it may improve the wanker's ethics. She chuckled, picked up her bags and headed down stairs.

Ness arrived in the hall just as Agnes was opening the front door to Kalum and Max. Leaving her bags by the foot of the stairs she called out a cheerful hello, Agnes ushered them in with her usual brusque frosty welcome.

"If you'll follow me, Sir John is waiting in the lounge," she turned to lead the way shooting Ness a look of contemptuous pity from under her lashes. She was sick of serving John, if only her husband had realised what he was getting them both into when he signed up for service to Moscow... had discovered too late it was his house, his name they wanted, not him... they made a plan; a trip to Scotland Yard to confess, throw himself on the mercy of British justice... hoping for leniency in return for vital information... he had gotten as far as the station when he was pushed off the platform straight into the path of an express. He had been mashed beyond recognition and John moved in a week later; Ewan and his blood lust soon after. The village thought she was still mistress of the house, John with his striking resemblance to her husband passed as his brother ready to take on the family legacy as Agnes had no children... she was sick of the pretence, the servitude, the blackmail and Ewan's sick, twisted blood lust. She opened the lounge door and stood aside.

"Your guests, Sir John."

"Ah thank you Agnes... welcome to my home," he stood and shook Kalum's hand, kissing Max on both cheeks. "Which would you prefer, tea then a tour or vice versa?"

Chapter Fifteen

The fate of a nation was riding that night.

– Henry Wadsworth Longfellow

Agnes stood in the doorway waiting an answer. Her thin bony arms pinned to her side, cheeks pinched, nobody could guess at the raging turmoil of hatred that was boiling in her thin chest. She seethed. His home! Welcome to his home!

Max took a notebook and a digital recorder out of her bag.

"I'd love a look around before tea if that's okay by everyone else?" She waved the recorder in the air. "Do you mind if I use this? If anything occurs to me it's easier to get the right sentiment across later when I incorporate the research into my book. Can I also take photos with my phone? I'd love a couple of the outside, the building is so gloriously Gothic." Max positively beamed at Sir John. She was passionate, excited and eager to gather as much research for her book as possible.

Ness looked at Max in new light. Fuck. If the woman wasn't a spy she'd make a bloody good actor.

John dismissed Agnes with the wave of a hand. "Tea later then Agnes, I'll ring when we're ready." He held out his arm to Max. "Allow me to escort you myself, dear lady... it is such a pleasure to meet someone with the same enthusiasm for great architecture."

Kalum and Ness followed behind as the party made their way outside. Ewan was closing the door to the cellar behind him as they entered the hall, John called out to him. "Ah Ewan, come and meet our guests," Ewan moved forward, his hand outstretched. Ness felt Kalum stiffen at her side. She glanced up at his face; he was smiling warmly, no outward sign of the revulsion she knew he felt, stretching out his own hand, he shook Ewan's long pale fingers firmly.

Ewan clapped his hands together. "How lovely! It's been ages since we've had guests for tea." His eye fell on Ness's bags. "I'll just put Miss Gordon's bags in the car."

Kalum stepped forward. "Allow me," without waiting for an answer he picked up the bags and motioned for Ewan to lead the way. Kalum followed Ewan around the side of the house to where the car was parked, leaving the others staring up at the gargoyles and turrets as Ness took photos on Max's instruction.

"Damn," Ewan fished in his pocket. "Silly me, I've left the keys inside… just leave the bags by the car and I'll see to them," he walked away. Kalum placed the bags by the car's boot. Unseen, he stuck the miniature magnetic tracking devices onto the metal brand signs fixed to the front of each piece.

Slipping his hand into his pocket, he triggered the corresponding receiver on his mobile; getting a small vibration signalling activation complete. Smiling, he joined the others. Ewan returned swinging a set of keys.

"May I suggest photos of the gargoyles on the left wing? They have a particularly nasty visage," the others assented and moved off. Ewan smiled maliciously at their retreating backs. While you do that I can safely take Miss Gordon's bags to the cellar; it's not as if she'll be needing them. Ewan was quick. Grabbing both bags and dashing to the cellar he hurried down the stairs through the secret corridor and into his own private lair. He looked around him with pride. His apparatuses gleamed under the bright lights. A shiver of anticipation ran through his body at the thought of his evening's entertainment and if all went well, if she was as strong as he imagined, the next forty eight hours would be the most glorious of his career. Pushing the bags to the side of the room with his foot, he left, leaving the big metal door ajar behind him. He didn't bother locking it... he would be back shortly.

Agnes stood in the shadow of the staircase. Watching Ewan with revulsion. Knowing what he had planned, that this miserable painful existence in servitude to evil and dictatorial masters was hers until she drew her final breath. She gasped and steadied herself on the wall. Sometimes she could feel her heart breaking. The feeling immobilised her. These monsters had no weak spots in their armour, no chink to aim an arrow at to stop them in their destructive paths. No way out. She straightened. Or was there? A memory began to surface through the pain, a conversation overheard between Ewan and Moscow. He was demanding they tell him the whereabouts of his father, he suspected they knew, why the refusal to divulge the information? He had slammed the receiver down and swore he would find out who the bastard was, would track him down and kill him. A slow smile crept along her thin lips.

The others came back into the hall. Agnes slipped silently behind the baize door as Ewan dropped the car keys into a bowl on the hall table.

Forty minutes later they reassembled in the lounge. Max was enthusing about the amount of material she had gathered... and all thanks to Sir John... he beamed at the praise. "It was my pleasure and now," he checked his watch, "I think it's time for tea... Ewan, would you kindly tell Agnes we're ready?"

"Of course. I must say, I'm feeling quite peckish," as he walked past Ness he reached out a pale hand and squeezed her shoulder.

Ness excused herself. "I'm just going out for a quick smoke," Max jumped to her feet. "I'll join you."

Ness and Max walked a little way down the drive. "You're doing well Ness…" Max took another drag on her cigarette before stubbing it out on the gravel. "… One last thing to do," she nodded to Ness. "It's time," Ness nodded, dropped her cigarette and ground it out under foot. She brushed the hair from her face and got it caught in her earring.

"Here let me," Max carefully took Ness' earring out, swapping it for an identical one hidden in her hand. "There is no way we are going to lose you Ness. We can hear everything you hear, we'll know where you are. Mark's in place, Ian's at the ready, okay?"

"Ready… let's get on with it."

***

They all sat around the lounge eating sandwiches and cake, smiling making small talk. John was puzzled, he couldn't understand what was wrong with Ewan. He had got his own way after all; the girl was his, there was nothing John could do about it.

Moscow had spoken and on their heads be it. Maybe he was just impatient for their guests to leave. John felt nauseous as he looked at Ness. Knowing in a short while she would be... probably best not to think about it. Glancing over at Ewan, he caught his eye raising an eyebrow in query. Ewan smiled unpleasantly and looked at his watch... so that was it, he was eager to get started and wanted John to say it was time to go. He drained his tea cup then cleared his throat.

"As much as I loathe to break up our happy party, it's probably time Ewan took Ness to the station," Ewan jumped to his feet. "I'll go and fetch the car while you say your goodbyes."

Ewan sat in the car, his hands gripping the steering wheel so tightly they hurt. He couldn't believe what he had been told... yet it had made sense. All these years he had begged for the knowledge and it was sitting under his nose all the time. Could she have been lying? But to what end? She stood to gain nothing from divulging her secret... she thought he had wanted to be reunited, needed to fill a void... thought if he knew he would spare the girl's life. She had been wrong on both counts. He imitated her high pitched pleading... Every boy needs a father, yours has been absent for too long and it's not fair, he has a moral responsibility... stupid bitch. He started the engine; he would deal with it on his return.

Pulling up to the front of the house he leant across the passenger seat and opened the door for Ness to get in. She slid into the car and buckled up. This was it, no changing her mind, no going back. Ewan tooted the horn as they passed Kalum and Max on the driveway, Ness waved. "They really are a lovely couple," she said to Ewan whilst looking in the rear view mirror. Kalum gave her a thumbs up: she had been heard loud and clear.

As soon as the car was out of sight Kalum and Max darted into the pines, heading back toward the house. They stood just inside the dark forest, watching the drive for Ewan's return. Dark storm clouds gathered above them, a rumble of thunder could be heard in the distance. Max looked up at the gathering storm and shivered; she hoped it wasn't an omen.

Ewan drove down the deserted lane, pulling into the side as the storm clouds burst. The sky blackened as the rain hammered against the car sliding down the windscreen like a waterfall.

Flake stopped the car with the engine running and turned to Ness. "I have a gift for you, but I didn't want to give it to you in front of the others. Close your eyes and hold out your hands."

Ness laughed. "Ewan. You shouldn't have," her heart was racing. Fuck, this was it... her voice sounded distant in her own head. Remember your instructions, don't panic... nobody was sure how Flake would knock her out; they had nothing to go on. The little redhead had been drunk, but Ness was alert and sober. She sucked in a breath and held it, closing her eyes and holding out her hands low on her knee, palms up.

Pulling a bag out from under his seat, Flake carefully lifted out a small bottle and a wad of cloth. Pouring the contents of the bottle onto the cloth he leant over with one hand, swiftly covering Ness' nose and mouth, pinning her arms to her chest with the other. She struggled briefly; her eyes flicked open in shocked surprise. Remember your instructions… don't panic… submit readily… the quicker you appear to pass out the better. Her struggle lessened, her body relaxed against the back of the seat. Eyes fluttering, lids closing slowly she went limp.

Flake removed the wad from her face and watched her silently for a few minutes. Ness slowly let out the breath she was holding until her breathing appeared normal. He leant close to her and she could feel his breath on her face.

"You and I are going to have fun…" he ran his tongue across her cheek. "I've waited so long…" He touched his cold lips to hers and sucking on Ness' bottom lip bit her hard… his sharp teeth sunk into her soft lip. She didn't flinch as a warm trickle of blood oozed from her lip ran down her chin and dripped onto her shirt. Satisfied she was out cold he stuffed the bottle and cloth in the bag and drove back towards the house.

From their hiding place, Kalum and Max watched Flake lift Ness' limp body from the car. A crash of thunder sounded overhead, followed by a crack as a large flash of lightening lit the dark sky, illuminating the car. Flake looked around him quickly before hoisting Ness over his shoulder and walking into the house. She felt slightly hysterical. It was all so 'Hammer House of Horror', she should have been wearing a long flowing white gown as the monster carried her into Dracula's castle. Making a circle with her thumb and finger she held it up as high as she dared and hoped they could see. Kalum radioed Mark.

"On their way."

"Got it mate."

Max scrutinised the second hand on her watch. When they looked around the cellar she had calculated Flake would need three minutes to get to the secret corridor carrying Ness. They would leave in two. She tapped Kalum on the arm. Unseen they darted toward the open front door and into the dim hall, silently making for the open cellar. They crept forward, knowing there wasn't much time before Flake made his way back up to close the door. Kalum went in front, Max following closely behind. He stopped and raised his hand, gesturing to his left. She took the left path and he took the right; by the time Flake came whistling into the dark dusty cellar both were hidden from view amongst the cobwebbed wine racks. He walked past their hiding places. As he disappeared from view they listened for the sound of his feet against the stone stairs. When Kalum judged him to be half way up them he motioned to Max through the racks to follow him. They made their way quickly and silently to the bookcase, pushing aside the sack curtain and down the secret passageway until they came to the shining steel door that looked so out of place. Max pushed on the door. It swung inwards. Stepping into the room with Kalum following close behind, both blinked in the bright artificial light. It rebounded off the shining steel surrounding them like a bizarre kaleidoscope. Taking up their positions from the plan Mark had provided, they lay in wait. Kalum looked over to where Ness lay on the table. She didn't move... he knew she was conscious; he had seen the signal she gave from Flake's shoulder. He puckered his brow. Everyone was in place awaiting the beast's return.

***

Flake stopped just outside the cellar door. He pulled it silently and turned the large ornate key in the lock. Taking it out, he pocketed it. The girl was out cold; he had felt his teeth go straight through her warm flesh... she wasn't going anywhere. He hadn't tied her up, just left her laying on his table... he wanted to take his time undressing her... relish in her vulnerability as he savoured the sensation of pulling the leather straps and steel locks tight against her silky skin. He laughed out loud, a high pitched laugh of elation full of expectation as he imagined her shock, waking up strapped to his table. He looked forward to the fear in her eyes, to her anguish as she begged for mercy and asked why? Why? They all asked that... why not? He always answered. The smile casing his pale face twisted. But first... first his father.

John was sitting in a high backed chair next to a roaring fire in the library, a large scotch in one hand, the decanter standing on a small table next to him. The curtains were drawn against the stormy chill evening and the radio was playing. Legs crossed, he tapped his feet in time to the tune. Flake quietly opened the library door. He stood watching John tilt his glass in the firelight, mesmerised by the flames dancing through the crystal... hatred surged through Flakes body... he stepped out from the shadow of the door frame and into the room, moving silently until he stood in front of him.

John looked up lazily from the fireside. "Yes Ewan? What can I do for you?"

Flake stepped forward and bent his long body over John's chair. When he spoke his voice was smooth, deceptively calm.

"You can start by telling me who my father is... I know you know his identity John. It's time you confessed... purge your soul."

"What are you talking about Ewan?" John sat forward in his chair and poured another scotch. "How many times do we have to go through this? I don't know who he was, how could we?" He leered up nastily at Ewan. He had had enough. Enough of Ewan's blood lust, enough of Moscow's indifference to John's fears, refusing to take his advice, heed his warnings... the scotch fuelled his frustration gave him courage to voice what he had been told never to disclose...he drowned his drink in one gulp before speaking. "When she serviced so many..."

Ewan's breathing was harsh; his sharp blue eyes bored into Johns. "You don't deny you are my father," he cocked his head on one side, one hand on the arm of John's chair, the other behind his back.

"I am not your father. I didn't take the opportunities offered... not with her anyway. And for the last time, I don't know who he was; none of us do."

Ewan leant in closer to John. He was almost nose to nose. "Liar," he hissed before drawing his hand from behind his back and plunging the knife deep into John's heart. He twisted the hilt making sure he destroyed his father's loveless lying core. He stood back, smiling, watching John jerk in the chair, liking the bewilderment on his face. Dipping his finger into the blood beginning to pool on John's chest he painted 'liar' on his forehead.

John's eyes widened in disbelief, his free hand went to the dagger and held onto the hilt. He looked down at it then back at Flake's face. It was a distorted mix of rage and joy as he smirked at John. "Night night... daddy."

The glass dropped from John's fingers rolling towards the fireplace, stopping in front of the fire. The orange flames sparkling through the crystal, igniting the covering of wet blood into a rich ruby red.

John trembled and became still, his open eyes glassy, staring, unseeing, into Flake's.

Flake straightened up, wiping the blood off his finger onto John's jacket sleeve. He felt cleansed. He'd always known his mother was a dirty whore. She was the same as the rest of them; lying filthy cunts, all of them.

He'd watched sometimes through the thin curtain that separated his mother's room from his and seen what they'd done to her. Holding her down while they entered her two at a time, laughing when she begged them to stop. He'd heard the men's foul grunting against his mother moans... occasionally one of the men would visit him while his mother was busy under a mountain of white stinking sweaty flesh. There was always extra money left on the table when that happened, more money for her to pour down her gutless throat. He'd put a stop to it; to her and the spawn she was carrying just as he had stopped his father's foul lies.

He stroked John's hair. "Miss Gordon is waiting for me, Father and we mustn't keep our guest waiting."

Flake left the room whistling. He had imagined this night for so long, he couldn't wait to get underway. He pulled the hair out of his pocket and sniffed... pity it had lost its scent. No matter, very soon he would have the whole thing... he licked his lips hungrily, his eyes burning blue lights in the dark as he made his way down the cellar stairs to his prize.

Chapter Sixteen

This animal is very bad; when attacked it defends itself.

– Theodore P.K

Ness lay on the cold table, unmoving. Her legs had lost the hollow jelly feeling caused by the chloroform... thank fuck she had held her breath. Even with the knowledge that the others had taken up their positions in the room she didn't fancy being out cold... if he had used a syringe she wouldn't have been able to do anything about it. Her lip throbbed painfully... could she risk stretching a bit? Better not. Flake had been gone a long time... what the hell was he doing? Just as she had decided to stretch her stiff legs the steel door opened and Flake came into the room whistling. She heard him walk over to the table, felt his hair on her face as he bent in close and kissed her swollen lips.

"So sorry for keeping you waiting Ness…" he tutted. "Very rude of me I know, it was most unfortunate but unavoidable." She heard material rustling as Flake moved around the table. "I had a meeting with my father." He stopped, and reaching out a hand, ran his fingers across Ness' breast. "The meeting didn't go well for him…" he sighed unconvincingly "… poor John. Still, he's in a better place now. Nothing to worry about any more… he was always so stressed; pressures of work I suppose. Vladimir will have to be told. He won't be happy… but he'll have another ready to take over from John, the operation will go ahead as planned… what's the worst he can do: sack me?"

He squeezed her breast hard before moving away from the table. Ness could hear him fiddling with equipment, moving something closer another further away. He came back to her. "I want everything to be perfect for us. You will look beautiful on film…" He laughed. "In fact, I have some footage of you. I know, I know; a little rude of me. First, let's get you out of these clothes and in a better position to enjoy the… em… proceedings."

Ness felt Flakes long cold fingers move against her chest as he began to slowly unbutton her shirt. Pulling her up into a sitting position by her shoulders, then with one hand gripping the back of her neck, he tugged the shirt off her arms. Laying her back down again he moved to the foot of the table and removed her boots, along with her socks. His fingers found the button of her jeans and soon they were undone, being tugged down past her thighs and pulled off.

"That's better..." His hand found her pubic mound and squeezed, kneading her flesh like a batch of dough. "... We can leave your undergarments on until I have you safely in position. It's more fun cutting them off. When you wake up I'll begin... I don't normally wait... but this is going to be so special."

Ness' heart was racing. She hoped they had recorded all of this because she sure as hell wasn't going to stay on this slab long enough for the bastard to chain her up. Ian had explained to her, they needed Flake to implicate that his Moscow boss knew what he had been doing in Britain, that he honed his bloodlust to serve them. Chains sounded above her, clunking together, moving slowly downwards... this is it, Ness, move your fucking arse.

As Flake grabbed Ness' left hand with his, the other pulling the chain down to shackle her wrist in the metal cuff, Ness made her move. As quick as a flash she felt with her right hand for the heavy studded knob of iron she had seen through half closed eyes as Flake carried her in. Gripping it firmly she swung the weapon in a wide arc, at the same time yanking down hard on the hand Flake was holding hers with. Relaxed and not expecting Ness to fight back, he was quickly pulled off balance. The heavy metal connected with his head as he stumbled sideways toward the table and fell to his knees, turning his face to Ness in disbelief before slumping to the floor, the chain swaying slowly above him.

Ness scrambled off the table dropping the iron on the floor. At the same time, Kalum and Max flew from their hiding places running to the table as Mark burst through the door leading to the kitchen stairway.

Kalum grabbed Ness under both arms supporting her as her knees buckled beneath her. Mark was at Flake's side in a flash, leaping over a fallen cabinet Kalum had thrown from his path as he ran to Ness. In one fluid movement Mark had pushed the unconscious but breathing Flake onto his stomach and stuck his knee into the small of his back as he pulled Flake's arms around and cuffed them tightly before yanking him onto his side. Didn't want the bastard choking on the blood pouring from his head. It had drenched the white coat he wore, pooling on the floor. Mark pulled his mobile from his pocket and dialled. He looked across at Kalum who had taken his jumper off and slipped it over his sister's head. She was sitting on the floor knees pulled up to her chest, head resting on one knee with her hand outstretched she was demanding a cigarette from Max in a shaky voice.

"Sir, we have him."

"I'll send the team in. Is Ness okay?"

"She's fine, Sir... smoking."

"Good work. See you all shortly."

The next half hour was chaotic. Within minutes of Mark's phone call, four large men had arrived through the kitchen into the cellar. They picked Flake up from the floor, wrapping him tightly in a straitjacket before loading him onto a stretcher. They left the same way they had arrived.

Another three came through with evidence bags and began to clear the room, taking photos of everything before it was labelled and packaged. Kalum helped Ness up and led her to the kitchen staircase, sending a meaningful look in Mark's direction, nodding toward the camera. Mark took the hint, removing the footage of Ness and slipped the film in his pocket. They sat around the kitchen table. Ness wrapped her hands gratefully around a steaming mug of coffee Max had made and lit another cigarette. Ian walked into the kitchen and sat down at the table.

"John's dead. Stabbed through the heart..." He helped himself to a cigarette from Max's pack and took a large drag before speaking again. "We have the evidence needed to prove Moscow's plan and the names of those involved this end. We'll pay a few well timed visits, present the evidence," he tapped the ash from his cigarette and pushed a sheet of paper toward Ness. "Read it."

She skimmed through the sheet, eyes wide in surprise. "Wow... shit... fucking hell..." looking up at Ian with a massive grin on her face she said, "but they're huge..." Her eyes flicked back to the sheet where household names of celebrities and politicians, to the less well known heads of forces and corporations were listed in black and white along with their own responsibilities in causing unrest within Britain and the EU... donations paid to the cause and money paid to them. She looked hopefully at Ian... "How much can I use?"

"First thing's first, Ness," he stopped, mid-sentence as an ashen faced Agnes was pulled in to the kitchen.

Ian motioned for her to sit at the table. She sat.

***

Two weeks later

Ness was curled up on her sofa watching the evening news. A newspaper lay next to her with the bold headline; JOURNALIST FIGHTS OFF SERIAL KILLER & FOILS BRITAINS COMMY COMMAND. By Ness Gordon.

Her exclusive published that morning had been timed for release on the day of the riots. She hadn't been allowed to use all the names on the list Ian had shown her; some of them, mostly politicians and big corporation heads, once presented with the evidence against them had broken down, confessed all. They had agreed to whatever they had been told to do. They had too much to lose not to. All of them were now under close observation, unable to travel outside the UK and constantly looking over their shoulders knowing their lives and their families were in danger from Moscow. It had been deemed not in the public interest to name them, for now. If they tried again they would be hung out to dry .The military and police would take care of their own traitors under certain guidelines. Those that had tried to run hadn't gotten far; they picked them up from airports, docks and a few private runways. They wouldn't be seeing daylight for a while. Probably wouldn't want to now, with their names being splashed across the media.

Her name flashed across the TV screen. Ness turned the volume up and leant forward in her seat.

Footage of people massing on the streets in London popped up. Their numbers were small; all of them were ordinary everyday citizens. There was some confusion as to the purpose of the day with some naming the EU, some benefit cuts. A few said they didn't know, that they had been paid to turn up and not a celebrity in sight. Most of them being holed up at home fending off the media that surrounded them. There was minor property damage and numerous arrests. Two murder charges in Glasgow and two in London, both stabbings. The culprits were now behind bars, protesting their innocence; they had been forced, threatened. Bollocks, thought Ness, they had been paid well to do a dirty job and end the paper trail.

The doorbell sounded. Ness turned down the volume and went to the door checking who was on the other side through the spy hole. Kalum had insisted she do this from now on and she wasn't to let anyone in she didn't know. He had been checking her compliance by randomly turning up for visits. Once in heavy disguise. Ness laughed at the memory and bent to the spy hole, Ian and Mark were on the other side. She took off the chain. "Hi. Come on in, go through to the lounge."

Ian smiled, patting her on the arm as he went past. Mark was incredibly sheepish; he tried to grin wickedly and finished up looking like he had a bad bout of wind.

Ness offered them both drinks. Ian shook his head as he sat in the armchair "Still working... Flake's dead," he waited for the news to sink in. Ness looked at him in astonishment.

"How?"

"This evening," he checked his watch, "One hour ago, at the moment the official version is massive heart attack. Unofficially we suspect Gelsemium poisoning... we'll know more after the post-mortem. We always knew this was a possibility, Ness... he knew too much to be left alone... we have too much evidence connecting him to Moscow. Plus he killed John. Acted on his own with no regard to his orders, threw a massive spanner in the works."

"How did they get to him, I thought he was under tight security?"

Ian nodded. "He was... a nurse administering his medication was an imposter with all the right credentials. Nobody questioned him, he went into Flake's room, administered the injection and left the premises. We have him on film but it's doubtful we'll see him again. Gelsemium poisoning is quick and deadly, causing massive heart failure... so unless there is cause to dig deeper," he shrugged his shoulders, "it happens."

Ness lit a cigarette and offered the pack to Ian. "Dead... gone where he can't hurt anyone again... I hope the narcissistic bastard suffered first, how's Agnes bearing up?"

"Remarkably well. She's a changed woman now she has her home back. Years of being blackmailed into compulsory servitude made her finally snap; she was terrified of Flake, sick of his evil craft. She was exceptionally useful, grateful to help in return for her freedom... as far as Moscow is concerned, John was alive and well carrying out their orders... Agnes simply pretended to be John. All correspondence was by post or courier and they were none the wiser. She has been advised to sell up and move on. The house holds nothing but bad memories for her. Flake's death should make up her mind; we'll take care of the sale and find her suitable accommodation elsewhere. We will, of course, remain in constant contact, for her safety as well as our country's."

"So that's it then… it's all over?"

Ian leant forward in his chair. "No, Ness… it's just the beginning. All we've done is throw a pebble in the pond and watch the ripples take effect. The threat to our country and Europe grows. There are dark days ahead; the shadow stretches across Europe once again, causing bitterness, resentment and conflict where it touches… it will try and creep under our door another time. What we have done is warn the people of its approach and given them enough evidence to make informed choices… if they were listening, they'll make the right ones. It's been seventy years since the last world war; not a long time. People are used to peace in Europe have forgotten the European Union covenants much more than a single currency, it keeps that peace flourishing… the next goal is simple: destroy the Union, destroy the peace."

Ness sucked in a breath. "So watch this space?" Ian smiled.

"Exactly." He looked at Mark. "Time we were leaving," they all stood and Ian made his way to the front door. Mark hesitated and turned to Ness. He ruffled his dark hair with a hand… opened his mouth to speak, shut it again and shrugged his shoulders. Ness watched him curiously. He bothered her every time she saw him… Kalum had since told her Mark wouldn't have harmed a hair on her head and reminded her, when she threatened to knee Mark in the balls next time she saw him, what was at stake at that time. She deserved what she got; Mark was no push over, don't think he wasn't dangerous… he was.

"If you have something to say, just say it."

"Ness…" He wanted to apologise, but Kalum had advised him against it… Hell, he'd never met a woman like her. He wanted to ask if he could see her again, take her out to dinner or a movie… he cleared his throat and thought, fuck it. Taking Ness firmly by the shoulders pulled her in tight to his hard chest, covering her mouth with his. She didn't have time to pull away and if she was honest, she didn't want to… Mark finally let go and before she could react pushed her from him and jumped through the open door way. "I'll see you at Kalum's birthday dinner next week," he pulled the door tightly to behind him and turned grinning to Ian.

"Ready to go, Sir."

The end